DANGEROUS FANTASIES

Book One

JESSECA JANAE

Dangerous Fantasies

Dangerous-fantasies-book-one.com

Copyright © 2022 Jesseca Janae Walker

DEDICATION

This Book is Dedicated to My First Born Son Josiah Obey. I started this book way before he was even thought of and I say that in the most humorous way. It was only after he was born that he gave me the drive, the motivation to continue and complete my first book. I wanted to give my son the world! Anything he set his eyes on, but with working a part time job on only a hand full of hours I knew It wasn't going to be an easy task. So every time he took his 30 min cat naps I would write and write until he demanded my attention by crawling over my laptop. Josiah this is to you Son! You showed me the true Meaning of Loving someone more than myself. You gave me more patience than I could have ever imagined of having. And for that son I Am Going to give you the World and everything it has to offer! I Thank GOD for Blessing Me with such a Perfect Mini Me. And Thank you for Blessing me with your Wild, Out of nowhere moments that keep me going every day! Keep Being you Baby Joe.

ACKNOWLEDGEMENTS

First, I would like to Thank GOD for blessing me with the motivation and willingness to keep going especially on my dark days. I've been blessed with so much support from family and friends throughout this entire process, the overwhelming feeling of joy is just coming at an abundance of over flow. To write the words *MY FICTIONAL NOVEL IS COMPLETE* feels like an achievement for us all! Of course, I have to give my individual and most important cred to My Family, I can't thank you guys enough for pushing me when I was too tired to push myself. Chiefy, Thank you for keeping the boys busy with nerf wars, pillow fights and dance off's all those late nights in the Crucial final stages of my book when I had my writing bug and couldn't be torn away for even a second. You wore many Hats, thank you. To Our Boys Baby Joe and AG you two Continue to be awesome! You guys literally get me out of bed every morning with just a flash of those Smiles and I'll forever be grateful my little munchkins don't forget you'll always have us and each other!

—With All My Love & Joy

Jesseca Janae

TABLE OF CONTENTS

CHAPTER 1:

JA'KAHLII

<u>2011</u>

When she opened her eyes, Jaz still had Dukes on her mind. She knew tonight she was going to give herself to him. That was what she said to Kacey, answering her question. "Do you really love him, though?" Cam asked Jaz, making her almost choke on her Jamba Juice.

"Of course, chick. Why do you think I'm making this decision after three years?" Jaz replied.

"Well, I still say you shouldn't. He's a lying, dirty-ass dog; once a cheater, always a cheater," said Kacey.

"Well, I love him and he loves me. I know he wouldn't even think about cheating." Trying to change the subject, Jaz picked up a pair of red stilettos out of her closet to go with the red lace panties and bra set she bought from Victoria's Secret earlier. She turned and showed her friends.]

"What do you expect, to be popping off tonight with them bad boys?" Kacey asked as she looked up laughing from the magazine she was going through sitting on the large white fuzzy area rug.

Cam agreed and listened with interest as she sat up right in jaz bed.

"Well, if you nosy tramps must know, my fantasy starts off with us in the kitchen. I'm feeding him strawberries with whipped cream, and he tells me to get on top of the table, so I do and lay flat. He then gets the whipped cream and makes a trail from the twins down to the kitty. Slowly, he starts licking each breast, determined to hear me moan, nibbling on them just hard enough for me to feel a tingle. Then, he follows the trail, licking every bit of my body. He reaches my pussy and goes head first without hesitation, sucking and tugging on my pussy lips. He goes straight for the clit, licking it just how I like it. I'm moaning and knocking everything off the table, trying to grab something, anything, to help me stay still. I feel myself about to climax, and he speeds up, looking up at me with determination. I scream, 'I'm coming, baby!' and bust all over his lips.

"Once he's finished licking the juice, he comes and meets me at the other end of the table. 'Let me have a taste,' I demand, trying to fight the urge to have some of Daddy's dick. I kiss him in a way that shows how bad I want him inside me. He picks me up and takes me to the bedroom. Usher is playing in the background. It takes him no time to take off his clothes. 'Come fuck me,' I tell him, spreading my legs across the bed, hands clenching the sheets. He does so, entering me. His pumps begin to get harder and harder, like he's trying to knock my pussy out. He goes deeper and deeper, just how I like it. I'm screaming his name, biting his chest, and scratching his back. The pleasure of just feeling his dick pulsing pushes me toward another orgasm. We both look at each other and climax together."

Jaz giggled as she saw the looks on Cam and Kacey's faces. "Uh, are you two okay?" "Are you sure you're a virgin? Did you tell Dukes about this? Is anybody else wet?" Cam asked.

Jaz started laughing harder. "Yes, I'm a virgin, and no, why would I tell him?" "Dukes doesn't deserve it. He might not even last two minutes with his toddler-sized penis." Kacey never had anything nice to say, but they all laughed anyway. "You've got a creative mind, Jazzy. Why don't you just write a sex story?"

"Nah, that's not me, Kacey. I'm going to be a dental hygienist, have a family, and no time for writing."

"Girl, I feel you," Cam agreed. "Well, we'll know what you're made of tonight, since my mom was able to get all our rooms so close on the same floor," Kacey added Later on, as the girls were getting ready for the champagne party, Jaz thought about what her friends said earlier about Dukes as she examined herself in her full-size mirror. He was a big flirt before he and Jaz started dating, and Jaz wondered if it were possible for him to change so quickly. There was a rumor about him and Danielle, a girl from her cheer team, hooking up, but there were always rumors about Danielle. She brushed it off with ease. She was ready for tonight, and nobody was going to ruin it for her.

* * *

Prom was the best experience of Jaz's life. Everything was going according to plan. She was dancing with the girls and they didn't want the night to end, but Jaz was getting nervous. She thought about how her friends had lost their virginity at fourteen, and they all said the same thing: *It hurt like hell.*

"Jaz, you okay?" Kacey asked as they waited for the limo.

"Yeah, girl, why wouldn't I be?"

"Well, you look like you've got something on your mind."

"Oh, no, just cold," Jaz replied. "Where's Cam?"

"She already left for the hotel with Romence. I thought they were going to have sex on the dance floor with the way they were dry humping."

Jaz laughed. "I didn't even notice she left. Where're Marcus and Dukes?" "They're probably in the bathroom, smoking their lungs away."

"Dukes's been drinking and smoking all night. We barely saw each other." Kacey gave Jaz that look; Jaz already knew she was talking shit in her head. Jaz tried to change the subject. "So, what do you and Marcus got planned?" "Girl, you know Marcus: we'll just argue, fuck, and fall asleep like we always do." "You say it like it's a routine and doesn't mean that much to you, Kace." "It doesn't, honestly, Jazzy. I'm not a virgin and haven't been for a while, so it's just another nut."

They started laughing when Dukes and Marcus walked up.

"What y'all chicken heads laughing at?" Marcus asked, looking higher than an airplane. "Not your broke ass," Kacey snapped back.

"You ready for dick tonight?" Dukes said to Jaz, grabbing her ass and trying to kiss her through his weed breath.

"Dukes, don't announce it to the whole senior class!"

"Oh, you don't want them to know you're still my little virgin?" His voice got louder. "You're drunk and pissing me off. I don't know why you like getting like this." Jaz felt irritated.

Just in time, their limo pulled up.

"You ready, girl?" Kacey asked.

"Yes, I am. Let's go!"

Once back at the hotel, before the girls headed to their rooms, Jaz and Kacey went to check on Cam to make sure she was okay. They knocked on her door, but there was no answer. They knocked harder until, finally, she answered. Her hair was wild, and the smell of weed wafted out of the room.

"What the fuck do you bitches want?"

They couldn't help but laugh.

"We came to check on you to make sure you didn't go into a sex coma," Kacey joked. "No, but Jaz, you need to get dicked down like me."

"I'm actually nervous, guys."

"Oh, here we go," Cam said, rolling her eyes.

"Dukes is wasted and already pissing me off."

"Well, you should have expected this," Kacey said.

"Get that pussy back in here so Daddy can have a taste!" Romence yelled from inside the hotel room.

Cam shrugged. "Well, I've got to go."

"Wait, what about my dilemma?"

"Look, Jazzy, either you're ready or you're not."

"Yeah, I agree, Jaz, and you know I never supported this from the beginning, so don't ask me," Kacey said.

Jaz groaned. "Man, you guys suck!" She shooed Cam away with her hand, a teasing smile on her face despite the nerves fluttering in her stomach. "Enjoy that dick in your mouth, Cam!"

They all laughed and retreated back to their rooms.

* * *

"Marcus!" Kacey yelled his name as she returned to the room, seeing him in bed asleep. "Marcus, wake your high ass up! All you do is smoke and drink."

Marcus laughed. "Fuck you."

"Boy, you can't handle me," Kacey said, shaking her ass in Marcus's face. "I'm about to shower and go to bed."

The hot water felt so good on Kacey's body, slithering down her smooth dark chocolate tattooed skin like Marcus' hands would. Mimicking what she could imagine him doing if he was behind her, she closed her eyes and slowly brought one hand up to pinch her nipple. Sucking in a breath, the other hand crawled down between her legs.

She got the urge to play with herself. She was so distracted with pleasuring herself she didn't notice Marcus had walked in and was watching her.

"Oh, without me? That's that shit Daddy don't like," he said as he pulled the shower curtain back completely, joining her under the warm water.

Kacey was startled and almost slipped.

"What are you doing in here, Marcus?" she said as she attempted to cover her body. "Well, if you weren't starting without me, you wouldn't have been so startled," he said admiring her five foot 3 petite frame. the small hawaiian flower on her lower back always turned him on, he gazed while massaging his hardening dick.

She raised a sultry eyebrow at him and smirked. "What, you think you're gonna get some?"

"Girl, *please*. Give me some of that."

She acted like she didn't hear him and began washing her curly highlighted sandy brown hair.

"Did this pussy miss me?" Marcus asked as he faced her, winding both arms around her. The suds from the shampoo slicked down her body, running over his hand, which was slowly making its way up to play with her nipples. The other hand sunk to her pussy lips.

By her body's reaction to his touch, he knew she was as ready for him as he was for her. Marcus slid two fingers between her pussy lips, moving them in and out. He teased her, knowing it would have her begging for him to pound her. He quickly turned her around to bend her over, inserting his dick without warning. It was rough, just how Kacey liked it. He felt himself about to cum, so he pulled out and busted all over her back.

After, they washed each other's bodies and headed back into the bedroom. All the lights were off, but Kacey noticed rose petals on the bed from the few flickering candles placed in the room. It was romantic, and even though he was a jerk at times, she knew they had a love for each other that nobody would understand.

Marcus laid her on the bed, but Kacey quickly got on top of him.

"It's my time to shine!"

She was ready to show him how much she missed his dick. Straddling him, she started to ride slowly until she got her rhythm.

"Ride that dick like a wild cowgirl!" he moaned as he gripped her waist.

She could feel his thick dick pulsing inside of her. When she felt him about to bust, his rhythmic moans becoming more frantic, she got up.

He blinked up at her, confused and irritated. "Why'd you stop, baby?"

"Because, baby, I want to please you in every way. You hungry?"

Before he could answer, she dipped her fingers into her wet pussy before placing them in his mouth. He licked with satisfaction.

"Tastes like candy, baby."

"How about the full meal?" Kacey asked.

He nodded his head. Before getting into 69 position, she reached for her purse on the end table and grabbed a tube of candy from the side pocket. She made a show of slowly unwrapping the paper of the red Starburst before inserting it into her entrance, nestling over Marcus' face so he could have full access to his meal.

While he was eating, she was only able to say, "Yes, daddy." She moaned, rotating her hips on his face.

Wanting the taste of his dick, she picked up another piece of candy and wrapped it around it, devouring it like a popsicle on a hot summer day. She admired the structure of his penis. She loved the small tone difference towards the tip of his dick, making it look larger than it felt. They both licked and lapped, Kacey barely finding coordination toward the end, but with one final suck, he exploded. Both collapsed, out of breath.

They cuddled up together, and before drifting off, Marcus whispered, "I love you, baby." Kacey smiled and fell into a deep sleep.

* * *

Meanwhile, Jaz paced her hotel floor in circles, debating whether she was ready or not. She finally decided she loved Dukes and wanted him to have all of her. She walked toward her room with confidence. Dukes was waiting for her—or so she thought.

As soon as she opened the door, she heard a woman's voice.

"You know I've been missing your big dick in my throat, baby. Why have you been keeping it from me?"

Jaz couldn't figure out whose voice it was, but she knew it wasn't one of Dukes' friends. She wondered if she had the wrong room. After stepping back to check the room number, she leaned in closer to hear their conversation.

"I can't believe you're still with that skinny virgin. I know she can't please you like I can."

"Look, Danielle, Jaz is my girl, and you're going to have to deal with it. You've been dealing with it this long, so shut the fuck up. You need to stop telling your friends about our quickies at school because if word gets back to Jaz, she'll be upset."

"I'm not worried about her. You're the only one scared of hurting her." Danielle sighed. "Look, I didn't come to argue, I came for some dick."

"Yeah, so hurry up before Jaz gets back with her friends."

Jaz tried to hold in the tears, but they started running like waterfalls. She became angry. The rumors were true, and her friends had been right the whole time. Jaz felt horrible for not trusting them and always defending Dukes' sorry ass. As she turned to run away, she heard Danielle moan and froze, anger boiling up in her. Whipping around, she lost it.

Jaz busted into the room, screaming! She ran to Danielle, who was positioned on her knees in front of Dukes, and punched her in the face.

Danielle screamed. "Get off me!"

"Jaz, stop! Get off her!" Dukes yelled as he stumbled to pull up his pants. The door bursts open again as Cam and Kacey rushed into the room. "We heard screaming! What's going on?"

They saw Jaz on top of a half-naked Danielle, and Dukes was next to them, trying to get them separated. Cam rushed over to Dukes and hit him, catching him off guard and knocking him off his feet. Kacey rushed Danielle and kicked her in the face and stomach. "Let the hoe get up!" Cam yelled.

They circled her, noticing Danielle's face was bloody and swollen.

Jaz turned her attention to Dukes, who was on the floor, holding his head down. "I hate you! I trusted you! You son of a bitch!" Jaz yelled and hit him.

Dukes was stunned by Jaz's strength and boldness.

There was more clamoring at the door, and three security guards surged in. "Hotel security! Ma'am, please put down the lamp or we will be forced to taser you!" the security said right before Jaz was about to break it over Dukes' head. The other security guards ran over to Kacey and Cam, pushing them to the ground and putting them in handcuffs, both kicking and screaming. "We wasn't done with that rat bitch!" Kacey yelled.

Jaz looked around at what had just gone down and dropped the lamp. The security guards put handcuffs on her as well, and they escorted them out of the room. Kids from school crowded the halls, already gossiping, and all she could do was glare back at Dukes knocked out on the floor and Danielle half-beaten to death. She was still bristling with anger and wanted revenge.

With a softer expression, she turned to her friends. "Thanks for having my back." "Anytime, Jaz. That trick had it coming," Cam said.

"Damn, we fucked that bitch up," Kacey said before laughing.

They couldn't help but all start laughing with her.

"I love you two. If I wasn't cuffed, I would give y'all a hug," Jaz said to her girls as they got in the back of the police car waiting for them outside of the hotel.

They weren't worried about being arrested; Cam's mom had bailed them out of jail within the hour, and they all crashed at her house.

* * *

Three months had passed since that incident, and it was now graduation. Dukes had been calling and texting Jaz every day since then, apologizing and begging her to take him back. *Of course he's sorry*, she thought to herself. *And that's all he will ever be.* Danielle's mom took her out of school that Monday after prom, fearing for her daughter's life. Her parents wanted to press charges on Jaz and the girls, but Danielle was too afraid to testify against them—she wasn't ready for another ass beating. Nobody had seen her since. Jaz was ready to put Dukes, prom, and high school behind her. All she wanted to think about was her future, and it started today. She walked across the stage with her best friends and let that chapter of her life close.

CHAPTER 2

LUNCH WITH A STRANGER

2021

"Ten-year high school reunion," she repeated out loud, sucking her teeth to the thought of seeing anybody remotely connected to that school. She tossed her phone down onto the table and picked up her glass of white wine, looking over the clear balcony view. "Excuse me, miss?"

Jaz was caught off guard, daydreaming while waiting for Cam and Kacey to meet her for their weekly lunch. She was glad the stranger approaching her didn't startle her so badly that she spilled her wine. She set the glass down on the table.

Jaz couldn't help but notice how handsome he was with his wavy hair, sexy dimples, and smile brighter than the sun. He was wearing the latest fashion trends, creating a fresh appearance she was impressed by.

"Yes?"

"I couldn't help but notice a beautiful woman sitting alone," the gentleman said. "Oh, I'm waiting on my girl-friends for lunch." She looked at her watch. "They're running a little late."

"Can I sit with you until they arrive?"

She shrugged. "Sure."

"My apologies; I'm Jamar," he said, extending his hand.

"Nice to meet you. I'm Ja'kahlii, but my friends call me Jaz."

* * *

Running late already, Jamar decided to stop and pick up some food from his favorite restaurant.

"Hello sir, welcome to J&J. Would you like a table for one?"

"No, not today. I'd just like take-out, please."

Jamar's phone suddenly rang. "Hello?"

"I already know you know who it is," Markel said on the other end. "My man, where you at?"

"I'm on my way."

"Well, hurry your ass up so we can go and handle this business."

"Alright, alright. I said I'm on my way," Jamar said before hanging up.

Shoving his phone back into his pocket, he turned back to the hostess.

"What would you like to order?" she asked, patiently waiting.

She stared at him, licking her lips. Jamar knew the affect he had on women. "Let me have the hot wing plate to go and a pink lemonade to drink."

"Is that all?" she asked, turning one corner of her lip up.

He knew she was flirting with him, but Jamar didn't like to entertain these young girls. He'd already done that in his college days, but he had graduated now. He was interested in real women. "No, that's all," Jamar said with a smile.

As he was waiting on his food, he looked to his right and saw a rare beauty sitting on the balcony, sipping on what looked like wine. She was alone, gazing out at the beautiful scene. The scenery at J&J's was always Jamar's favorite part. The restaurant was settled right near the water on top of the Heaven Hills Way, 30th floor. *Above the clouds*, some would say, with large windows practically the size of the wall that gave everyone a glittering view of the swaying ocean. He didn't want to waste this opportunity. He quickly walked up the stairs. "Excuse me, miss?"

"Yes?" the attractive women replied.

He could tell he caught her off guard.

"I couldn't help but notice a beautiful woman sitting alone."

"Oh, I'm just waiting on some girlfriends for lunch." She checked her watch. "They're running a little late."

"May I sit with you until they arrive?"

He was nervous, which wasn't normal for Jamar. When he approached women, he was confident, and knew he had the best game in town.

She smiled. "Sure."

He was taken in by that smile, but he quickly regained his senses when he realized an awkward few moments had passed and he was still standing. He shook his head. "My apologies; I'm Jamar," he said, extending his hand.

"Nice to meet you. My name is Ja'kahlii, but my friends call me Jaz."

"What a beautiful name. It's unique; I don't think I met anybody with that name before."

"Well, that makes two of us."

They both laughed.

"Go ahead and have a seat." She motioned for him to sit.

"So, Jaz, do you always come here?"

"I do, occasionally. What about you?" Jaz asked.

"Yeah, I come here quite often. It's one of my favorite places." He looked out from the balcony. "Best views in town."

"I've never seen you here before," Jaz said.

"Business had me overseas last spring. I can tell you really like this place, though." "How'd you figure that?" Jaz asked.

"Well, see, I'm the type of guy who can get all the information I need from observation." "Okay, then tell me what you have observed so far about me." Jaz smirked. "Well, first off, the waiter asked if you wanted the usual, and I saw you have a membership card dated back to 2009." He tilted his head toward the window. "And it's a beautiful view like I said. You've been sipping on your wine and looking over like it's something that keeps your thoughts intact."

Jaz laughed. "Okay, some of that's on-point."

"I haven't taken my eyes off of you since I walked in."

"So, you were watching me from a distance like a stalker," she said with a devious smile. "Well, with your beauty, I wouldn't be shocked if you had a few stalkers," Jamar responded. "The difference between me and your stalkers is, once I caught a glimpse of you, I actually introduced myself instead of just watching and catching blue balls." They both laughed.

"So, tell me about yourself, Jamar." Jaz twirled her hair. "Are you from around here?" "I used to be, but I'm just back in town on a business trip.

"What kind of business?"

"I'm a defense attorney. The clients I represent pay me a lot of money to get them out of the hot seat."

"The way you're dressed, I thought you were a drug dealer or hustler." Jaz immediately covered her mouth. "I'm sorry, that was rude of me to just blurt out."

"It's okay." He laughed. "But what's wrong with the way I'm dressed?"

"Honestly, nothing—everything looks good." Jaz eyed him up and down as she sipped her wine seductively. "It's just that most people I know don't have the new Jordans on before they come out, or wear a couple of hundred dollars' worth of accessories. You like to spend money on yourself, and there's nothing wrong with that."

"Wow, you're a woman with a good eye for jewelry and fashion. I guess I'm not the only one noticing things," Jamar said with a sexy smirk. "How old are you, Jaz, if you don't mind me asking?"

"Why would I mind?"

"Well, my mom told me asking a woman her age is rude."

"Yeah, some women think that, but I don't mind. I'm twenty-seven."

Jamar appeared shocked, eyes widening. "Really?"

"Yes." She smiled. "How old do I look?"

"You look that exact age. Career choice? And before you come back at me, I'm just asking because the way you carry yourself makes me think boss."

"I'll gladly accept your compliment because I am, indeed, the head bitch in charge." She giggled. "I'm the lead dental hygienist and the youngest in my office."

"Sounds like you're at the top of your game." He sent her an impressed smirk. "I'm glad you notice a real woman when you see one."

Before he could respond, the waitress sauntered over with a filled plastic bag, purposely standing between Jaz and Jamar. "Here's your order, sir," the waitress said, cutting off the conversation purposely.

Jaz shot her a nasty look.

"Will you be needing anything else?" the waitress asked flirtatiously.

"No, that's all," Jamar responded, turning back to Jaz. She smirked at the way the waitress frowned before turning back to her duties.

"So where were—"

"Hey, sorry we're late, Jaz. Traffic was so bad," Kacey said as she approached the table, Cam trailing behind.

"Oh, you already replaced us?" Cam asked, laughing

"No, not at all, ladies. I just wanted to keep her company until you two arrived," Jamar said, getting up and pulling out some chairs for them. "My apologies. My name is Jamar," he said before he returned his attention back to Jaz. "Well, you're in good hands now. It was very nice to meet you." He kissed her hand. "We'll talk soon," he said before walking away with all the confidence in the world.

CHAPTER 3:

JAMAR

Jamar tapped on the steering wheel as he waited at the red light, the low music overpowered by Markel's complaining.

"Aye, bro, don't ignore my calls. What if there was an emergency or I got kidnapped or jumped?" Markel went on like he always did, but Jamar was barely listening. He was thinking about how beautiful Jaz was. Something about her interested him. She was different and exciting. He wanted her in his life.

Markel snapped his fingers in front of Jamar's face. "Are you okay? You seemed distracted."

"Yeah, I'm good. I just met this unexplainable girl today at J&J's."

"The new waitress?"

He snorted. "Hell no, not her. I've got socks older than her! I've never seen this woman before."

"Oh, so that's why your ass was late? Over some pussy, bro?"

"No, she's not like that. She seems different than the other girls I fuck with." "You sound real whipped already, man."

They both started laughing.

"Tell me about her," Markel said as they slowly approached a large gate.

"Another time," he said with a wave of his hand. "We're here, so get your game face on." Jamar rolled down his window as a guard approached his car. "I'm here to see Mr. Pierce. Tell him Brooks is here."

The guard backed into the booth and made a call. Jamar could hear him telling whoever was on the other line who he was and what he was there for. Jamar glared in his rearview mirror, noticing three men surrounding the back of his truck with canines. As the guard continued on the phone, two more approached the rear doors with AK rifles. Markel started to tense up, feeling uneasy. He reached for his 9mm under the seat, but Jamar stopped him with a firm hand on his arm, all the while never taking his eyes off the guard in the booth.

"Don't wet your pants," the guard near his window said behind the glass. Markel was ready to hop out, but he knew they were there for business and had to stay professional.

The guard hung up the phone and leaned out of the booth. "Mr. Pierce has been waiting. Follow the trail and it will lead you to the house."

Jamar rolled up his window with a nod and drove up as the gate opened.

"Look, Kel, if you want to do this business, you need to be smarter about your actions and cooler on your temper."

"I was just taken aback by those damn dogs. I can handle it," Markel snapped back, feeling belittled.

"That's not an excuse. This line of work we're in requires you to be ready for the unexpected. You show an ounce of weakness, and anybody can and will take your life. You're going to be seeing wild and insane shit soon, trust me. Just let me know if you can't handle this, because I need to trust you to keep your emotions under control."

Markel knew everything that Jamar said was true and for his own safety. He nodded and kept silent.

"Stay ready so you never have to get ready," Jamar said as he finally reached the top of the hill, where a large mansion sat nestled in the countryside. Parking in the rounded driveway with an angelic water fountain in the center, both men got out of the ghost-grey, sleek SUV and approached the grand, golden double-doors.

* * *

Back at the restaurant, the girls were interrogating Jaz about the man.

"Ja'kahlii Eynett Evans, who the hell was that sexy guy you were sitting with?" Cam asked, already poised in her chair for the gossip.

"Honestly, I don't even know him, girl. I was sitting here, waiting on y'all, and he just walks up to me out of nowhere, introduces himself, and from there, we started talking." A slick grin escaped her lips

"Well, I know I'm not the only one who noticed how handsome and well-dressed he was," Kacey said.

"Uh, yes, I noticed, along with those pussy eating lips," Cam added, dramatically fanning herself.

Jaz rolled her eyes after they all giggled. "It doesn't matter how cute or well-dressed he was; it takes more than that to get these panties wet."

"Yeah, yeah. You've been saying that about every guy you've met for the last year, Jaz. Get over that shit. Just because you had that one-night stand doesn't mean you should base all future relationships on that," said Kacey as she placed her hand on Jaz's shoulder in a supportive gesture. "You just weren't ready for that, and you did just break up with that dude, Glen."

"It's like one minute you were going heavy, then the next, you guys broke up. We should have known that going from something consistent to nothing would have a toll on you," Cam added, nodding as she agreed.

"It's not like that!" Jaz said defensively. "Look, I knew what I was doing with that guy." "Well, if you knew what you were doing, then how come you haven't had sex in months? What, is your pussy under lock and key now?" Cam asked sarcastically then sighed. "I guess it's either that or handing out your pussy to every dude with a nice car and a little change in the bank." She sent a pointed, teasing look at Kacey, who laughed.

"There's nothing wrong with being spoiled by a dude," Kacey said.

"Yes, I agree," Jaz said. "There is nothing wrong with a guy spending his money on me, but that doesn't automatically mean he's getting this kitty—unless he's earned it." She splayed her hands out like she was presenting something. "Then I shall bestow on him something that will change his life."

Cam laughed, swatting Jaz's dramatic pose away. "This bitch thinks her pussy is made of gold or something."

"Who's to say it isn't?" Jaz teased to the amusement of her friends. The girls sat for another two hours gossiping and catching up before gathering their things to leave. "Alright, ladies," Jaz said, "I have to get back to work. I have a consultation at four. Let's get the check and go."

"Yeah, I'm with you, Jaz." Cam checked the time on her phone. "I have to go pick up Kylee and Kaylee from daycare."

Kacey let out a giggle as she sat back and viewed her friends.

"Look at us—Jaz, you're the youngest hygienist in your office. Cam, you're the mother of two beautiful girls, and you're almost finished with your veterinarian degree. I'm an ER nurse! Who knew we would get this far in life?"

"I know! That's the truth, girl," Cam agreed.

"Well, I always had faith in us. I knew we would make it. And we're still making it! Give me a hug, ladies, and let's toast to us."

They raised their glasses.

"To us!" they cheered.

"Excuse me, miss," the waiter said, interrupting the girls cheers. "Here's your dessert." "Oh, I didn't order any dessert." Jaz blinked in confusion at the covered plate in his hands.

"The gentlemen you were sitting with earlier paid your tab and said to send this over once you asked for the bill."

The waiter placed the mystery plate on the table and lifted the cover from the plate to reveal an Oreo ice cream cake—Jaz's favorite. It had a note next to it that read, "*I hope you enjoy this dessert as much as I enjoyed our conversation. Here's my number, just in case you get curious*," signed by Jamar.

Cam clicked her tongue. "No man has done that for me before."

Kacey nodded, agreeing with her, while Jaz picked up the note with a smile before leaving the table. If he didn't have her attention before, he certainly had it now.

CHAPTER 4:

CAMERON

Opening the door with her daughters on her heels, Cam heard a familiar voice from the kitchen call, "Hey, honey, how was lunch with the girls?"

After all three put their stuff down by the door, the two little girls yelled, "Daddy!" They ran to Sean with the widest open arms, jumping on him for their famous bear hugs and kisses. "How're Daddy's favorite girls?"

"I missed you, Daddy," Kylee said.

"No! I missed you more, Daddy," Kaylee said.

"I missed you both more than you missed me. How was school? What did you learn today?" He asked question after question as he tickled them and made fart noises on their cheeks.

"Great, Dad! We played on the slide and in the sand-box," the girls said in unison. "That sounds fun. Now, let's go start your homework. Daddy will be in there to help in a moment, okay?" he said as he sat them down from the counter.

"Okay, Daddy!" they chirped and then raced to their room.

"Now, back to my favorite lady." Sean hugged Cam around her waist. "How was your day, beautiful?"

"Oh, it was great, Daddy!" Cam laughed as she mimicked the girls. "No complaints, and lunch with the girls went well, as usual."

"Anything new with them? I know there's something with Kacey. That girl always has something going on."

Cam threw a light punch to Sean's arm. "Leave my girl alone. She's just very active. She's been through a lot."

"Yeah, a lot of dick!" He snickered, and she chuckled under her breath before poking his chest.

"There's nothing new with her, but there is with Jaz!" Cam was excited.

"Oh, go ahead, girl, I'm listening," Sean said, mocking the way Cam talked on the phone. "Well, Kacey and I were running late to lunch because there was a shoe sale—"
"Oh, so that's where that four hundred dollars from my account went."

"Babe, stay focused," she said, sidestepping the shoes. "This isn't about me, it's about Jaz. So, when we finally met up with Jaz, she was sitting with a man I've never seen before. We come to find out she didn't know him either, but that's not even the juicy part. Before we left, the waiter walked up with a dessert and a note that said the sweetest thing along with his number." "Yeah?"

"And once we were about to pay, we find out he paid our entire bill already and gave us roses. Well, *Jaz* got a dozen roses, but she shared. I gave it to the girls, who trampled it when they got out of the car."

"Our dainty girls," he said with an amused smile. "I'm glad I saved some money on the credit card then. I think I like this guy already," he joked.

"Don't worry, honey, you're the only man who can spend his money on me." Cam kissed him, running her hands down from his chest until one was massaging his penis. "Let's get a quick one in, baby, while the girls are busy doing homework." Despite his heavy breathing, he grabbed her wrist and said, "No, you know the girls will be running in here any—"

"Daddy! Daddy! I need help!"

The girls ran in right on cue.

"Exactly," he said with a sigh before addressing his daughters. "Okay, here I come." He hugged his wife and whispered in her ear, "Before this night is over, you'll be calling me Daddy again." He smacked her ass and walked away.

* * *

"That shower is just what I needed. I just wish I didn't have to put away these dishes," Cam said to herself as she walked down the stairs toward the kitchen.

To her surprise, the dishes were washed and food was put away. Come to think of it, she didn't hear the girls fighting over anything or any of the TVs on, either. A look of concern crossed her face. She found a note on the counter that said, *"Ol' dude isn't the only one that can leave notes. Tonight is all about you, baby, as soon as you find me."*

Cam smirked. She felt her panties get wet and started her search in the living room. She went upstairs to the bedroom, but there was nothing. She rushed down to the laundry room and back up to the attic—also empty. Tapping her foot on the floor like a four year old, she began to get irritated.

She decided to take a shot of Patron to calm her nerves from the high cabinet in the kitchen, then two more as quick as she poured them—she decided the first one wasn't going to help. After the fifth shot, she heard some music coming from the backyard. She tiptoed to the curtain to see what it was.

Cam was shocked to see her husband, with white roses and lilies and wine on ice, sitting in front of the projector screen, and playing her favorite movie on the white sheet he had hanging on the back fence. She tried to get herself together as she walked out to the back. She knew she loved him more than she could explain—he was *her hero, her soulmate*. She began to cry. Sean rushed to her.

"Baby, what's wrong? Are you okay? What happened?"

All she could do was hug her husband, burying her face into his shirt. Sean pulled her chin up and wiped her tears.

"What's wrong, Cameron?"

"I'm fine, I promise," she replied.

"Well then, why're you crying, crybaby?" Sean joked.

"You just make me so happy, and I love you," Cam said.

He grinned. "You just realizing that now? Is that why you were crying? You just realized after seven years you love me?"

"You know what I meant, jerk." She flicked his ear. "Kiss me and shut up." They kissed passionately, and Sean's hands began to explore Cam's body like it was the first time, migrating one down to sneak underneath her pants and taking a handful of ass into them. He found his way between her legs and felt her freshly waxed vagina. "Somebody's already wet for Daddy."

He massaged her pussy, as Cam moaned into his ear. Their breathing got heavier, and although she wanted him to finish, Cam removed his hand. Bringing him down to the leopard print blanket, she laid him on the ground and climbed on top of him.

"How much does your dick miss me?" she asked. "Has he been missing me, baby?" She reached through his sweatpants and pulled his thick, hard penis out, taking it all in her mouth with one motion. She began to deep throat him, bobbing it in and out of her mouth with swirling licks of her tongue. His moans became louder.

"Just like that, baby. Keep going." He felt his knees becoming weak when she reached his sweet spot under his nut sack of gold called the *gooch*. He could never resist when she licked with the tip of her tongue and blew cool breaths there.

Sean aggressively sat Cameron upright, motioning her to spread her legs so he could devour her pussy, licking all the right spots. She was barely able to keep her legs from shaking. Sean smacked her ass.

"Put that dick back in your mouth."

She did as instructed, getting back into a rhythm and feeling his dick hit the back of her throat as he sucked on her clit. With that burst of pleasure, she gave one expert lick, and their movements become frantic before they both climaxed in each other's mouth, swallowing it all and not wasting a drop. The dogs next door started barking, waking up the neighbors. Cam came harder than ever.

"Let's go inside, baby, before the neighbors come out," Sean suggested, shimmying his pants back up his waist.

"Fuck 'em. This is our property."

Sean chuckled but ignored his wife and picked her up. He carried her upstairs to the shower, intending to finish what they started.

CHAPTER 5:

KACEY

What do they have that I don't? Why are they all so effort-
lessly happy, and I'm not? They've always had what I've
wanted. When will I be happy? Kacey repeated to herself
as she drove home from the thirteen-hour shift she worked
at the hospital. Memories from her past started crossing
her mind. She heard the screams from her memories as if
they were happening again, and tears formed in her eyes.

* * *

One of these memories started like another normal
day. Kacey woke up that morning and got ready to hit the
streets with her friends. As she entered the kitchen, she
noticed her mom wasn't up cooking everything in the fridge
like she normally did on Wednesdays. She paused, resting
her purse on the kitchen island, daydreaming. She was
taken out of her thoughts by Jaz honking from the street

loudly and rudely. She brushed off the bad energy that came across her and grabbed a Pop Tart out of the pantry, just before rushing out the front door.

"Bitch, what took so long?" Jaz asked. "I know your mom had to be on your head this morning 'cause your timing is real disrespectful." Kacey shot her the stank face before getting into the all-white Jeep Cherokee with gold trim.

Ja'kahlii rolled her eyes at her friend before she pulled onto the road, swerving in and out of traffic irresponsibly. She sped into a semi-empty commercial parking lot like she was auditioning for *the Fast and the Furious.*

The girls walked toward the only pink building on the lot. Once inside, they scanned the room until they saw Cameron sitting alone in the corner and joined her.

"Yo, wassup? Why you guys late? We almost missed our reservation," Cameron said angrily.

Jaz shot Kacey a pointed look. "Ask your friend. This bitch's been acting weird since I picked her ass up."

Cameron knew when something was up with her best friend by the way she didn't have a snappy, sarcastic remark for Jaz's comment. Before she could give it any more thought, a blonde-haired older lady with blue highlights through her messy bun came from behind the receptionist desk. "We're ready for Waters, party of three.

Is your party here?" "Yes, we're here and ready!" Ja'kahlii said, nearly jumping out of her seat.

Cameron bumped Kacey's shoulder jokingly so they could make fun of their best friends' excitement. Kacey jumped up too and said, "Yes, let's get these vaginas steamed and cleaned." The receptionist was excited to see the girls' responses. She walked over and opened the door leading to the back and beckoned them to follow. The girls were given each their own dressing areas.

Cameron slipped into Kacey's changing station, startling her. She tried to quickly cover her half naked body.

"What the fuck, Cam? You ever heard of knocking, beyotch?!"

"Don't act like I ain't never seen you naked," she joked as she took a seat on the tiny stool in the corner. "But seriously, Kacey, what's going on? I've noticed you been distant since you guys arrived. Did something happen this morning with your Mom? Was she off her boat again?"

Kacey put her head down and turned to face the mirror behind her as she let out a sigh. "Cam, I didn't even see her this morning. I've been trying to replay the last time I've even seen my mother." She tried to calculate the exact days since they spoke. "We were texting a few days ago before I went and spent the weekend with Marcus. I snuck through my bedroom window this morning like normal, but she wasn't asleep in my bed waiting for me, nor did she blow my phone up bugging about where I been."

A look of confusion came across Cameron's face. "Well, that's a good thing then, girl. She probably got called in for an earlier shift this morning or something and didn't have time to get on your ass."

"Cameron, you're not hearing me." Kacey turned back around back to face her friend and started shaking.

"I haven't seen my mother in days. She's been getting sick lately. I haven't even been checking on her, and I've been so wrapped up with Marcus drama. I have to go find her." Cameron became increasingly worried for her friend. "Kacey, what do you mean she's been sick? Is she using again? Has she been hitting you? Talk to me, girl. You're scaring me. I'm going to go get Jaz."

Cameron turned towards the door, but Kacey instantly became frantic. She grabbed Cam's wrist before she could leave the dressing room.

"No! Don't go get her!" Her voice cracked with every word. "She's been stressed enough with her own problems. I don't want to add mine to the mix. Besides, you're probably right, Cam. It's flu season and I'm just overthinking this. My mom will be home by the time I get there with a story about the bitch that works on the floor above her." Kacey tried forcing a smile for her friend.

Not convinced, Cam decided to leave it alone like her friend asked. "Alright, just let me know if you need anything, Kacey, okay? Please don't leave me out in the dark. You're my sister, and I'm here for you." Cam Hoped she believed her concern was real, extending her arms for a hug. Nodding in agreement, Kacey embraced her friend before wiping her tears.

As the girls began their session, Kacey listened to her friend's ridiculous laughs and crazy stories. She was able to relax for their woman's day. She cleared her mind of all doubt, knowing her mother was okay and for the first time in months, she looked forward to getting home to her and asking about her day.

During their steams, the vaginal masseuse offered unlimited shots of sake, which Kacey and Ja'kahlii took advantage of. By the end of the session, the girls felt recharged, revamped, and tightened. Cameron decided to be the designated driver when she saw Jaz and Kacey go toe-to-toe with all five shots, toasting to everything.

Pulling up to Kacey's home first, since she was the closest drop off, Cam helped her stumbling friend to the front door. She used her spare key to let them in. Upon entering, the entire home was dark and cold, like the air conditioner had been on for days, which felt unusual to Cameron. She knew they didn't have AC, and Kacey's mom always kept a light or two on just in case Kacey came home late. Before Cam could say anything about the lights and the cold, Kacey began slurring words.

"Damn, its dark as fuck, and it's been cold like this for days now. When the fuck is my mamma gone turn on the fuckin heater?"

Jaz began honking the horn a ridiculous number of times. Cam left Kacey on the couch with a blanket, waste basket, and water before running back to the truck.

"What the fuck is your problem, Jaz? You know these old fuckin' pigs over here will call the cops on us, and if we get pulled over, I'm going to kill you."

"Calm down, Cam. I was just trying to get your attention and tell you to take Kacey to Marcus's house. She been staying out the house on purpose. Her mom's been using again, and she was so out of it a few weeks ago that she even asked Kacey to join her." Jaz slurred her words but kept eye contact with Cameron the entire time. "She came to my house crying and shaking like she had seen a ghost. She begged me to not call you or come by." Jaz threw her head back and dozed off.

"How could she not tell me? Why would she keep us away? We've always had her back since day one," Cameron said to herself as she looked back at Kacey's front door. She felt glued to her seat, afraid to face what she might find at her friend's house. She decided to not face her fears and just hoped for the best. Thinking about how Kacey wanted them to trust her when it came to her mother, she said a prayer and focused on getting back to Jaz's place safely.

* * *

Kacey jumped awake, gasping in fear on the couch. She could've sworn she felt a cold hand and even colder breath on her.

"Mom? Was that you? Are you here?"

Looking around and grabbing her arms, she got up from the couch and walked toward the lights in the kitchen, flicking all of them on and off to see if the electricity was out. None of them worked. She mumbled under her breath and rummaged through the kitchen cabinets until she found a couple of candles and matches. She set them around the house and checked her mom's room, but it was locked. She finally took her cell phone out her pocket.

"Los Angeles KB General Hospital, Trauma Unit. Where can I transfer you?" "Hey, Liz, Its Kacey, Karen's daughter. Can you transfer me to her office, please?" The nurse on the other end paused before gathering her words. "Kacey, where have you

been? I've been trying to reach you for a week. The house phone is disconnected and the number

I had for you was no longer in service."

Suddenly getting a chill across her body, she sat on the other end of the phone, confused. Kacey ignored the nurse's questions, repeating herself.

"Liz, where's my mother? Let me speak to her."

She seemed hesitant to respond, but finally said, "Kacey, I'm sorry, sweetheart, but your mother is gone. Her body was found a few days ago. They said it was a suicide." Liz's words became fuzzy in Kacey's ears. Her eyes swelled with tears, her chest felt like a huge boulder had just been dropped on it, and her knees began to buckle.

"That's why I've been trying to call you nonstop. I've even been by the house a few times, hoping to catch you."

Kacey couldn't believe what she just heard.

The silence began to scare Liz. "Kacey, sweetie, where are you? Are you still here?" Clearing her throat, some words finally escaped her mouth. "Elizabeth, tell me exactly where she was found."

Because of her tone and use of her full name, Liz knew Kacey was serious. "She was found by people walking by. Her body was in some tunnel passages near 38th and Western, over in the thirties hood. The old gangsters used to call it the catwalk. It's on the opposite side of town. I'm sure you're not familiar wi—"

"Nah, I know that area very well. You and my mother used to cut up them rocks and sell pussy over there with them pimps."

Liz was silent, caught in her shock by the words coming from Kacey's mouth. She began to stutter. "E-Excuse me, I beg—"

"Nah, bitch, you heard me," Kacey said, cutting her off mid-sentence. "I know that area, and I know all about you introducing my mother to that shit all them years ago. I'm going to get to the bottom of this, and if I find out you had anything to do with this, I'm going to take everything from you," she said before launching her phone against the wall, causing it to shatter into pieces. She screamed out in hurt. Her screams pierced her neighbors' ears.

Liz sat on the other end, still holding the phone with the dial tone in her ear, and became frantic and nervous. She looked around to see if anyone heard or was watching her. She began packing her desk in a hurry and headed to the employee lounge with her purse.

Another nurse saw the worry in Liz's eyes and came over to her. "Liz, what's going on? Where are you going? You just clocked in. Are you okay?"

Without a word, Liz hurried passed her to the service elevator that was used for emergencies and out the back door without a word, disappearing into the thick fog.

Kacey sat in the kitchen with her head down for some time thinking of her next actions. A voice whispered, "Let's kill them all." Grinning from ear to ear, Kacey agreed.

* * *

Snapping back from her flashback, she wiped her tears. She was so deep in her thoughts she didn't notice she went thirty blocks passed her street and ended up in a rough-looking neighborhood. She tried looking for a familiar street, but the dark skies and shot-out street lights made it hard. She decided to try and make a U-turn, but a guy stumbled toward her car at the light and approached her window. "Miss!"

She ignored him, gripping her wheel.

He banged on the window, hard. Three more guys appeared from the alley and approached her car as well.

"Now that my homies are here, you have two options. You can open the car and you won't get hurt, or you gon' *make* us open it," the thug said with vicious smile on his face. Kacey reached slowly to unlock the door, heart hammering in her chest.

"Hurry up, bitch! You're starting to piss me off!" he yelled, and she flinched. Finally, she opened the door.

It swung open. "Now, how hard was that?" He reached in the car and grabbed her breast through her shirt.

Kacey tried wiggling away as she began to cry and scream for help.

"Shut up, bitch," he said and smacked her across the face.

This is the end, Kacey thought. *Maybe if I beg him to let me go and give him all my money, he will let me go.*

"You're coming with me," the thug said.

"No, please," she begged. "Just take the car and my money. I won't say anything to anybody, I swear," she pleaded as she tried to escape his grasp.

"Bitch, the homies are already taking all that. I'm taking you!"

Kacey screamed louder.

"DJ, fuck that broad, kill her, and dump her body down the street," his friend chimed in. Her body trembled. "No, please, I'll do anything. Don't kill me!"

DJ got turned on by the way Kacey begged for her life.

"Don't worry, baby. I'm going to have some fun with you before I let you go." "No, please!"

He smacked her across the face again, and she yelped.

"Shut the fuck up. You're annoying me now."

Kacey continued to cry.

DJ leaned further into the car and smashed his fist into her face, and she felt a gush of blood fall down her now-broken nose. She didn't even have time to scream as he punched her again, again, and again until her vision blacked out.

He threw her bloody body in the back seat like a sack of laundry and sped off. Later, only half conscious, she felt her body being dragged, her feet scrapping against cement. She was barely able to see, but she could tell she was being carried into a dingy house covered in trash, something quickly pierced her rib cage as she was dragged through the last room and was thrown on a bed that smelled like old rescue animals and death. Out of the corner of the one eye she could use, she could see DJ getting undressed, tossing his shirt in the corner. Unable to move her broken body, she began praying for forgiveness for all the wrongs she'd done in her life.

I'm sorry for sleeping with my best friend's husband. I'm sorry for sleeping with Dukes in high school.

Suddenly, gunshots rang through the house. DJ tensed, pulled out his pistol, and ducked next to the window across from the door. He heard footsteps outside, so he shot toward it, hoping he hit his target. He walked toward the door slowly.

Bang! Bang! Bang!

The bullets tore through him, and his body fell to the ground. As he attempted to stand back up, he lost his balance, teetering, until he crashed out the window.

"Check every room in this house, and then burn it down!" a deep voice yelled from the hallway.

"Come look at this." Two guys walked into the room and saw Kacey bleeding heavily, hovering over her. Their voices swirled around her, and she could barely tell who said what. "She's barely breathing but still alive. Should we just leave her?" one man said as he looked to the other for confirmation.

"I say we help end her suffering." The man with a thick gold rope around his neck said as he cocked his pistol back and pressed it to her left temple.

"Yo, TC, come here and help these guys search the house," the first man yelled as he pointed out the room toward the hall.

"Doc, how's she looking?" the assertive male asked.

"If she doesn't get help soon, she will bleed out."

"Alright, pick her up and bring her with us—she might know something." One of the guys went to the window and saw only blood; there was no body. "He got away. He couldn't have gotten far. Go! Go find him, now! We're done here. I got

what I needed, so burn the bodies. I know somebody heard these gunshots, so we have to get out of here."

* * *

Jaz felt anxious as she dialed *his* number while sitting on the counter of her kitchen. It rang and rang, but just as she was about to hang up, someone answered.

"Hello?"

"Oh, hello. Can I speak to Jamar?"

"Well, hello, Jaz. Yes, you may."

"How'd you know it was me?"

"I'd recognize that voice anywhere."

"How are you doing?" Jaz asked.

"I'm doing great, beautiful. How about yourself?"

Jaz heard someone screaming in the background, and she furrowed her brow. "Am I interrupting anything?

"No, not at all. I can talk."

Suddenly, the screaming stopped, and Jaz was nervous all over again.

"So, about that question—how are you?"

Shaking her head to get rid of that feeling, she said, "I'm doing well, no complaints." "Good, there shouldn't be any."

"Oh, there shouldn't, huh? What if I had all the problems in the world? Would you fix them for me?" Jaz teased.

"Normally, I'd need to know what I'm getting myself into first. I'd need to know what the stakes are and if the case is worth my time and skills. But for you, it would definitely be worth looking into."

"What if it became something serious? Maybe life or death?"

"Well, Miss Jaz, you don't seem like the type to get into that kind of trouble, but if you trusted me and gave me the truth, I'd save you."

"This is getting pretty deep for our first phone conversation. You sound like Superman saving Lois Lane."

"With my job, I always give my all—nothing more, nothing less. But enough of the hypotheticals, Jaz. What are you doing right now? Are you busy?" Jamar asked assertively. "No, I'm just at home, waiting for the sun to set."

"Well, how about you get dressed and meet me somewhere?"

"Well, I—"

Jamar cut her off. "Great! I'll text you the address. Meet me in an hour. I'll see you soon," Jamar said before hanging up. She blinked down at the phone before darting to her closet to find something cute.

* * *

Jaz waited anxiously. She looked out at the ocean, feeling the breeze on her skin. "I'm glad you could meet me here so last minute," Jamar said from behind her. She turned around with a smile.

"Well, I wasn't doing anything major. I just hope I wasn't keeping you from anything important. You sounded busy when I called."

"Never too busy for you." He winked.

She tried to hide her flushed cheeks by gesturing to their surroundings.

"What are we doing at the beach in the winter?" Jaz asked. "I love the beach, but it's a little nippy."

"I thought you'd like it."

"Oh? How did you guess that?"

"You admired the view at J&J's. I knew you could relax and appreciate this one a little closer."

"I never thanked you for buying me and the girls lunch the other day. We appreciated it. Next meal is on me," Jaz said.

"So, there's going to be another date?" Jamar asked.

"Date? I said meal. Who said that was a date?"

"Well, this here is an official date," Jamar pointed out. Jaz thought his voice sounded sexy, the way it brushed up against her ears gently like the tides behind her. "So, what would you like to do on this official date?"

"Get to know each other," she suggested.

"Take a walk with me." he asked politely.

They slowly made their way down, passing by empty docks and seagulls flying by. "Tell me about yourself, Jaz. What's your family like?"

Jaz started shivering.

"My bad, I didn't even notice how cold it was. I have two sweaters and a scarf on. Would you like my jacket?" Jamar offered.

"I would love a jacket."

Jamar wrapped her in his jacket, and she took a good sniff of his Chanel Bleu cologne, which she liked.

"So, back to my family question…"

"Oh, yes, I'm an only child. My mother raised me on her own after my dad was killed in a drug deal when I was five. My mom was kind of into thugs." Jaz laughed. "Don't think I'm laughing at the fact my father died, but I never really knew him, so I couldn't feel much for a stranger anyway."

Jamar waved her off, snorting. "Did you just quote Tupac?"

She grinned. "I didn't think you'd catch on to that."

"Who doesn't know Tupac?"

"Yeah, you're right." Jaz looked out at the clean brown sand across the beach. It was almost empty due to the season, except for a lone boat bobbing against one of the docks. The colorful, bright phoenix painted on the side caught her attention.

"Wow, look at that beautiful boat. I've always fanta-sized about getting on one of those, drifting out to sea, and enjoy the sunset from the ocean."

"How come you haven't?" Jamar asked.

"It's not the cheapest thing to do."

"I'd imagine it would be if you knew somebody who owned one."

She chuckled. "But I don't have any rich friends."

He hummed in acknowledgement before changing the topic. "What fascinates you about the beach, Jaz?"

"To some people, the beach is one of the dirtiest, most crowded places, but I find it calming. I like the way the sky never ends, how the waves never stop, the breeze forever blows. It makes you think about how things in life could be beautiful forever. When I have problems, I come to the beach and just stare at the sky and breathe. I feel like all my problems disappear as quickly as they came. I see everything clearly." Jaz sighed and turned to Jamar, blushing when she saw him looking at her. "What are you staring at?"

"You, and how beautiful you are when you talk about what you're interested in. Come on," Jamar said and grabbed her hand, leading her onto the boat.

"Wait, we can't be on here. What if the owners come back? We could be in big trouble." "We'll have it back before they even notice."

"I don't know about this, Jamar."

"Look, Jazzy, if we get in trouble, I'll get us out of it. It's my job, remember?" Jaz was still unsure.

"Do you trust me?" Jamar asked.

She hesitated before nodding. "Yes."

Without another word, Jamar started the boat and sailed off.

Where the fuck did he find the keys? And how did he find them so fast? she thought to herself. Jamar stopped the boat just past the one-mile marker so they could watch the sunset, just letting the boat drift. By the end, Jaz no longer felt guilty for borrowing someone's boat—this moment was all worth it. But just as the sun dipped into the ocean, sirens from a nearby Coast Guard approached the boat.

"Jamar, the Coast Guard is coming. The owners probably reported the boat stolen." "I'm coming!" Jamar yelled from below deck where he went to check for drinks. "This is the Seal Beach Coast Guard. Do not turn your motor on or attempt to flee. Stay where you are."

"How could I be so stupid?" Jaz asked herself.

"Ma'am, please state your name," the coast guard said as they came up to the boat "Ja'kahlii Evans, sir."

"Well, Ms. Evans, local residents said they saw you and someone else boarding the boat and believed you were stealing it. Does this boat belong to you?"

"No, sir."

"Is there anyone else on this boat, ma'am?"

"Yes, he's below deck."

"Sir, please come from below deck with your hands up," the coast guard said through his intercom.

Jamar came up the stairs slowly with two glasses of champagne and a rose. "Mr. Brooks, I didn't know it was you," he said with a note of surprise in his voice. "Some of your neighbors reported seeing two people board your boat earlier. I'm guessing they didn't know it was you. Sorry about this," the man apologized.

Neighbors? He lives over here? This is his fucking boat? This mother fucker. She had a million thoughts racing through her mind.

Jamar nodded. "I appreciate you coming to check out the situation."

"No problem, sir, you have great night. Ma'am, you do the same." He tipped his hat to Ja'kahlii before steering off.

As soon as they left, she whirled around and yelled, "Are you fucking kidding me!? This is your boat? Asshole! You damn near gave me a heart attack with those sirens." Jamar placed the glasses down and walked up to her, placing his arms around her small waist.

"Jaz, don't be mad at me. I didn't want to ruin the surprise. We were only going to have a walk on the beach, but the way you talked about the sunset and how you wanted to do this one day made me want to see that through for you. It wasn't planned at all, then I couldn't pass up the look you gave me when you thought it was stolen." He laughed before grabbing her face and looking into her eyes. "I will never put you in a situation I can't get you out of. Do you trust me?"

Without hesitation this time, she said, "Yes."

"Great! Now, are you ready for your surprise?"

"Wait, what surprise? Jamar, I can't accept anything from you. I—"

He placed his finger over her soft lips. "Just accept this rose and follow me," Jamar said, leading her below deck.

Her eyes lit up from how amazing it looked below. A table was set with color changing candles, appetizers, and champagne on ice. In the corner was a heart-shaped bed with rose petals over the comforter.

"Oh, Jamar, this is beautiful. Is this what you were doing down here? It's too much, especially since you barely know me."

"Look, Jaz, I noticed you don't like being catered to or shown any type of interest through gifts, because you feel you don't need a man to buy you anything, but let me tell you this: I do what I want and will buy you whatever I want if I decide to. I did all this tonight because I wanted to show you how much I liked the way you took a chance on me and how you've been honest with me. So, sit and let me show you how much I appreciate it." "You're not going to ask me to marry you next, are you?" Jaz joked.

"Oh, no, I haven't picked out your ring yet." Jamar laughed. "Now, if you don't have any more questions, can you please join me for dinner?"

"Yes, I will."

She turned around and hugged him.

CHAPTER 6:

THE PAST

"Mommy, Mommy, wake up." Kaylee and Kylee rushed to Cameron's side of the bed. She rubbed her eyes and sat up, yawning. "Look at what we made for you," they said, each holding onto an end of a tray of food.

"I thought I smelled chocolate chip pancakes and eggs. Thank you, girls. You two are the best!" Cam said, hugging her girls.

"You have to thank Daddy too. He made the coffee."

"Where is my big boy so I can thank him with a kiss?"

"He left, Mommy," Kylee said.

"He said to give you this paper, Mommy, and a bunch of kisses," Kaylee added as she handed her mom a note.

"Oh, he did, huh? Well, where are my kisses, munchkins?"

She smothered her girls with affection. Seeing their smiles and hearing their laughter made Saturdays one of best days of the week.

"Okay, Mommy, that's enough kisses; our show is on."

"Do you want Mommy to turn on the TV for you?"

"No, we're not babies anymore, and Daddy already turned it on for us." The girls giggled and raced out to the living room.

She gazed at the note left for her. It took her back to times her and Sean ran the streets. *Dangerous days, fast times*, she thought to herself. She felt her stomach drop. This was it. Their past had finally caught up with them.

Good morning beautiful. I didn't want to wake you— you were sleeping so peacefully. I have to run a few errands. I'm not sure how long it'll take, but I made you and the girls some breakfast. There's $100,000 in the safe, gun loaded. I love you always, and I will see you and the girls soon. Sean.

Tears rolled down Cam's eyes. None of what Sean wrote was new to her, but she always hated the possibility of never seeing her husband again. They had more than enough in their safe to run away from their old life and start a new one, but Sean had wanted to stay in his fast life of delivering drugs and making money.

When they first started their deliveries over five years ago, before their family, she felt a rush every time. After that one dark day, she knew everything she needed to know about him and was ready to ride or die. She used to help Sean on his regular money pickups for Mr. Simmons. They'd drop off the packages, pick up cash, and then deliver it back, just like clockwork. Sean introduced Cam to his lifestyle early on in the relationship.

Flashbacks began to run through her head.

"Who's the woman?"

"I was told there was only one person working for Mr. Simmons," an Italian boss said to Sean.

"This is my assistant, if you must know. Look, we didn't come for conversation, just money," Sean replied as he tossed the duffel bag of money at his feet.

"You better watch it when talking to me, boy." He lifted his gun to Sean's chest. "Now here's the new deal: you're going to go back and tell Mr. Simmons he owes my boss five hundred thousand dollars for the shipment he lost. Until then, we're keeping our money and the next shipment. Oh, and your little assistant is staying here with us."

Feeling her chest becoming heavy, Cam scooted out the bed, placing her breakfast tray on the nightstand. Her memory became more and more clear.

Two of his men stood at the door, cocked their guns, and stood ready.

Cameron looked at Sean with tears in her eyes. She should have listened to him and stayed her ass in the car.

Suddenly, in swift movements, Sean pushed Cam down and pulled his two Glocks from his waistband to fire at the men. Cameron screamed, covering her head as she hit the ground. She could hear glass shattering and bodies falling.

Once the shooting stopped, Sean ran to Cameron. "Baby, get up. Come on, let's go! Get the bags and let's go."

The overwhelming feelings from those moments now overcame her body, making her knees weak just like it did back then. Even after all this time, the memory of so much death still haunted her dreams. The girls singing along downstairs to their show helped ground Cam again.

"Wait, Sean, you're hit."

"Don't worry about it; I'll be okay. Hold the gun and just get the bags. Don't touch anything else."

She did as told, but as she went to run out the door, the Italian boss appeared again, placing his pistol to Sean's head.

"You thought you were going to get away with this, you little punk?" He cocked his gun back, ready to pull the trigger.

Cameron closed her eyes, breathing irregularly.

There was a bang, and the Italian boss dropped to the floor before she even registered that her gun had gone off. His body layed there, leaking, soul leaving.

"Cameron, baby, are you okay? Give me the gun," Sean instructed as he grabbed the shaking gun from her hands.

"H-He was going to k-kill you," she stuttered in disbelief. "I had to do something. I-I'm sorry." She began crying uncontrollably.

He grabbed her shoulders tightly. "Look, baby, we don't have time for this; the cops will be here any minute. You did what you had to do. They would have killed us both. It's okay, let's go!"

They ran out of the warehouse to the pickup truck and sped off like bats out of hell. Red and blue lights flashed in their rear view, accompanied by the shrill of the sirens. Once they reached the hotel, they locked the door, closed all the curtains, and hid the gun under the fireplace.

Sean called Mr. Simmons to explain everything once he counted the product and cash he collected. Cameron couldn't take it. Her head felt like it was spinning. She ran to the bathroom and threw up everything in her stomach. The smell of blood was on her. She felt it in her hair, under her nails. She couldn't believe what just happened; she had just killed someone. No amount of showers would make her feel clean again.

Sean opened the bathroom door. Through all the steam, he saw Cameron sitting on the shower floor, holding herself, head buried in her legs. He stepped in and sat behind Cam, pushing her short curly black hair out of her face as he guided her head to rest on his chest. The showerhead rained over them.

"Baby, it's going to be okay. It's all over now. We're safe," he said as he massaged her temples.

"Sean, I killed a man! I took his life! You killed those men! It wasn't supposed to happen like that. They're not going home to their families." She continued to cry. "Look at me, Cameron," he said, lifting her face toward his. "They were going to take you! They would have killed you! I know how these men work, and I had no choice. I wasn't going to let that happen to you. What we did was self-defense. You didn't take a life, you saved mine. I am forever grateful." A rush of affection overwhelmed Sean. "I love you, baby. I will protect you forever. We can get out of town for a while if that will make you feel better, baby. We can go wherever you want, just us two."

Cameron nodded. "I love you, Sean. Promise you'll never leave me".

He hugged her tighter. "I promise," he said and kissed her forehead. Chills overcame her body.

Cam snapped out of her memory when she heard the girls downstairs fighting over the remote.

"Give it to me! It's my turn!" she heard the one yell.

"No, it's mine!" the other said, followed by a smack, thump, and the sound of glass shattering.

She put her mom face back on, wiping away her tears.

"What's going on down there?" she asked from the top of the stairs.

The girls turned to Cam and raced to snitch first.

Cam couldn't do anything but laugh as she saw the frame encasing a picture of her mother-in-law broken on the floor. She never could stand her. Once she reached the bottom of the stairs, Cam got the broom and dustpan and began sweeping it up.

"It was trash anyway," she assured them.

CHAPTER 7:

YOU. ME. US.

The room felt like it was spinning as Kacey's eyes adjusted to the light. She tried to move her wrists, but she noticed she was handcuffed to the bed. There were voices coming from the other side of the door. She tried to speak, to get their attention, but her jaw was still swollen and sore from the punches. She hit the bedrail with the chains on the cuffs, but no one came in the room. She layed there, crying and drifting in and out of sleep from what she assumed was a drug. "Hey, miss, can you hear me?"

She could hear fingers snapping near her face. She wasn't sure how long she'd been asleep, but when she opened her eyes fully, three men stood around the bed. One of them wiped her face with a warm towel.

"Are you okay? Do you feel dizzy?" he asked as he checked her heart rate. Kacey began to focus, gasping.

She sucked in a shuddering breath as she took in her surroundings. It looked like this room was a bedroom if the dresser, end table, and bed she was currently on said anything.

"Take it easy. You've been in and out for two weeks. I've been taking care of you. You had a concussion and a few bruised ribs. You were beat up pretty bad," the man closest to her said.

Kacey flinched in discomfort. "Why does my head feel like this?"

"I gave you some heavy meds to help with the pain. That feeling will go away soon," the same man replied.

"Who are you guys?" she asked, looking around at the group of men.

"My name is Doc, but people call me DC."

The other men remained quiet and stared at her. A fourth man, however, suddenly came in and pushed DC aside.

"Let me talk to Li'l Mama alone. You guys go check on the order," the man said. Kacey recognized his voice from the house they'd rescued her from.

The men did as told, but one gave her a devilish smirk as he closed the door behind him. "What's your name? What were you doing in that house? Did you know any of them?" He fired question after question at her. "You want those cuffs off?" he asked once he noticed the bruising it caused. "You seem like the type to enjoy them," he joked but removed a small key from his pocket.

"Under other circumstances, I wouldn't mind," Kacey said as he removed them, and she massaged her wrists as she sat up.

"So are you ready to tell me about—"

Kacey cuts him off. "Look…uh, what's your name?"

He raised an eyebrow. "It's Markel—Kel for short."

"Okay, Kel, I know you think I know something, but I don't. I'm tired, and my face hurts right now. I need a hot bath and some food. Please, just let me go home. I promise I won't tell anyone anything."

Kel smirked. "You know I can't do that Li'l Mama. Tell me your name."

"It's Kacey, and I was kidnapped the same night you came to that house." "Well, I'm sorry to hear that, Kacey, but you can't leave until I get what I need." Markel snapped his fingers and two men came into the room.

Her heart pounded, and she leaned away from them. "Please don't kill me. I don't know anything, I swear."

"I believe you," Markel said as he walked out the room, answering an incoming call on his cell. Yeah, Q, she awake…" was the last thing she heard before he disappeared behind the door.

The men picked her up, and Kacey kicked and screamed as she was carried through the house, down to the basement, where they sat her on a bed.

"Are you going to kill me?" she cried.

"No, you dumb broad," one of the men said angrily.

"Aye, cool it, Roc," the other said.

"Sorry," he apologized to her. He was a tall, husky, strange man, but he had a warm smile as he said, "My name is JB. This is Kel's guest room. He told us to bring you here so you could shower, eat, and get some rest. The bathroom's through the doors on your left. There are new clothes on the bed and food in the kitchen. If you need anything else, just knock, and one of us will get it for you."

They left and closed the door behind them. Kacey was confused but accepted the chance to shower and eat anyway. She got off the bed slowly. The first thing she noticed was how elegant the space was. The art on the wall showed taste. The eighty-inch TV and seven-foot aquarium showed the owner had a "big man" complex. She chuckled as she walked around, admiring everything. The basement was spacious, almost like an apartment to her. She wandered around into cabinets and closets, going through all the drawers, looking for something to help her escape. She needed a plan, but decided to take a bath first. She sat in the oversized jet tub and thought to herself, *I know the girls are worried about me. I don't even know how long I've been gone. A week at least, I guess.*

"Fuck those bitches!"

Kacey jumped out of the tub and whirled her head around the bathroom.

"Who's in here? Who said that?" She grabbed the shampoo bottle as a weapon, as if it would help her defend herself.

"You know who I am," the voice responded back.

She was scared, but she knew she recognized the voice.

"You're not real! You're not real!" She kept repeating to herself as she covered her ears, trying to drain out the voice she heard.

"I'm as real as the hate we have for them. You know those hoes don't care about you like I do, baby. All they care about is themselves. They shove their success and happiness in your face! But me, I've been here for you since the beginning, humbled."

She raised her head with a devilish smile. "You're right, they don't love me—they never did. We should have killed them a long time ago, like you said. It's their fault I got kidnapped. I hate them!" Kacey screamed at her reflection.

"Don't worry, baby. Their time will come. We need to figure out how to get you out first, then we will handle them," the voice continued.

She looked in the mirror and smiled at herself.

* * *

Cam's phone rang, Jaz's name flashing on the screen, so she set her book down next to her on the bed and accepted the call.

"Hey, Cam."

"Hey!" Jaz said.

"Have you talked to—" they both said at the same time.

"Girl, I'm worried," Cam said. "I haven't seen or spoken to Kacey in—"

"Yeah, me too," Jaz agreed. "But we know Kacey. The last time this happened, she was just on a bender in another state."

Cam laughed. "Yeah, you're probably right. I'm sure she's okay." There was a pause

before she continued. "So, last time we talked, you rushed me off the phone because you were on a date with that guy. When you didn't pick up, I got nervous. I was just calling like you told me to. I wanted to make sure you didn't get kidnapped."

Jaz chuckled. "Well, I appreciate it."

"You appreciate it? Girl, start spilling the juice! What happened? Where did he take you? What'd you guys do?" Cam demanded answers.

"I was definitely blown away." Jaz sighed dreamily. "It was the best first date I've ever been on. It's been weeks now, and he's still so consistent and such a gentleman. Remember when I told you he said to meet on the beach?"

"Yeah?"

"So, I was really nervous. I thought about how many ways he could get rid of my body if he killed me there."

Jaz heard Cam laugh on the other end of the phone. "You're so dramatic." "Anyway, we met up and ended up on this boat, and sure enough, he didn't kill me. We fucked all night," Jaz said

"Wait! What? You two ended up where, doing what? He owns a boat? What exactly does he do again, Jaz? He's not another Melvin, is he?" Cam had so many questions. "No, Cam, he's not a drug dealer. At least, I don't think he is," Jaz said, laughing. "I'm just surprised you didn't text me to call and save you like you always do. You didn't even call me once you got home. You were too busy having sex with strangers. Are you sick or something, Jaz? You want me to come over?" Cam was baffled.

"I'm fine, girl, really," Jaz promised. "I'm just trying something new."

"Bitch, you're just fucking something new."

They both laughed.

"Now, tell me, how was he? Did you cup his balls while swallowing like I showed you? You ride him backwards cowgirl?"

"Mommy, what's backwards cowgirl?" Kaylee asked, head popping out from under the bed.

Cam gasped and pulled the phone away from her ear. "Kaylee! What did I tell you about eavesdropping on private conversations?"

"Kylee, come on, get out." Kaylee crawled out, pulling Kylee with her. They ran out of the room before Cam could smack them.

Cameron picked up the phone again, and Jaz sounded like she was out of breath from laughing so hard.

"Oh, shut up. I can't wait until you have some of your own."

"Damn, I love my god-babies," Jaz said. "I have to go, though, Cam. I have a new patient coming in soon. I'll call you later."

"Yeah, you better. You know I need to hear the dirty details."

"Yeah, I know you're nosey. That's where your daughters get it from."

"Bye!" Cam said and hung up.

* * *

"Ms. Evans, your one o'clock is here."

"Okay, thanks, Angel. You can send them in," Jaz told the secretary.

Her back was turned to the door as she finished setting up. She could hear when her patient walked in.

"Welcome! You can come in and have a seat. I'll just be a minute."

She heard the door slam and a cold piece of metal push against the back of her neck. "Turn around, bitch."

As she did, a hand smacked her across the face twice, and she gasped. "What the fuck?" "You're as bold as you are pretty," a girl with tear-drop tattoos on her face said. Her accomplice, another girl, walked up to her. She was smaller and prettier than the other. Jaz could still smell the fresh press from her scalp, and her pedicure she left the tissue between her toes.

"So, you're the bitch he's been talking about," she said to me in a soft, rhetorical voice. Jaz flittered her gaze frightfully between the two women. "What are you talking about?" She hit Jaz across the face with her gun while the other girl punched Jaz in the stomach

until she fell to the floor. They both kicked her until they were out of breath. Angel, who heard all the commotion, knocked on the door.

"Ms. Evans, is everything alright? Why is the door locked? Are you okay?" She banged on the door, but when no one responded, she said, "I'm calling the police. Security is on their way."

They ignored Angel and knelt down next to Jaz. The pretty one moved her hair out of her bloody face with her gun.

"Stay away from him," she said. "Or the next visit won't be so pleasant." Both of the girls jumped out the window seconds before security broke through the door. Angel gasped when she saw Jaz bloodied on the floor. "Somebody call an ambulance!" she screamed to the security guards.

After the ambulance and police came, they questioned her about what happened. She truthfully didn't know, *who could have sent them? what were their motives? Could they have meant Jamar?* thinking to herself, but agreed to file a report and give what details she could.

"I'm sorry this happened to you," Angel said, looking regretful and small in the uncomfortable hospital chair next to Jaz's bed. "I should have been there with you." Jaz shook her head. "Don't blame yourself, Angel. You couldn't have known this would happen."

"Please let me take you home. The officers said your car was vandalized, and the tires were slashed."

Her chest tightened at that, but she still smiled at Angel. "Thank you."

On the drive home, Jaz sat in the passenger seat and tried to figure out who could've done this to her and why did they go through so much trouble. The only thing that came to her mind was Jamar.

* * *

"He said I could leave days ago, but my spirit feels like a weight to his. I feel as if only he understands me. He understands us!" kacey kept talking to herself as she curled her hair in the mirror, getting ready for her dinner.

"You looking good already, baby," he said as he kissed her behind the ear and cupped her exposed breast. She let out a giggle.

"You became comfortable with just walking in here while I'm getting ready." "Yes, I have. You've became comfortable with staying after I told you weeks ago you were free to go. Tell me why you stayed?"

Staring into the mirror, feeling weak and ready to confess her love for him, she then looked away with her blushing cheeks. Her phone began to ring.

"Go ahead and answer the broad, keep being her friend, and keep focused. That nigga Jamar gon' get his too!" he whispered in her ear and gripped her hair, causing her to yelp in discomfort.

"Hello, Jaz are you okay? Slow down. Tell me what happened. I'm on my way." Rushing out the door, she jumped into her purple truck, ready to track down the two girls who hurt Jaz.

* * *

Later that night, Kacey started cleaning her gun with a look of satisfaction as she thought about the lifeless bodies she threw into the water with cinderblocks tied to their ankles. She wiped away the DNA left on it from pistol wiping the girls. It gave her a rush. Her devilish grin worried Cameron. She looked back over to Ja'kahlii as she paced back and forth around their hotel room, eyes wired open and biting her nails.

"You two are completely insane! What the fuck happened back there? We need to talk about how that went that wrong!" Cam shouted.

"Look, you screaming is not helping. Take one of these and come sit the fuck down," Kacey said casually as she threw a sandwich bag full of narcotics at her.

"We were only supposed to jump those bitches, not commit double homicide!" Cam jumped off the bed hysterically.

"You need to chill, bitch! The moment you panic, we're caught! Sit the fuck down!" Kacey jumped in Cam's face.

They begin a screaming match.

Ja'kahlii finally snapped out of her trance seeing her girls folding under the pressure, and turning on each other made her angry.

"Both of you bitches are acting like kids! Cam, come here. What happened has already happened! We can't go back and change anything now," Jaz said as she held her crying friend tightly to her chest.

"Yeah, tell her again" Kacey said sarcastically as she went back to the gun. Jaz helped Cameron to the other full-size bed in the room before she turned her attention to Kacey.

"Bitch, you aren't excused for your dumbass actions! It's your fault it got out of hand! You didn't have to shoot them, Kacey. You went too—"

Kacey snapped at her, getting in her face. "Don't forget you called me to ride with you, Jaz. You called me crying, ready and down for whatever, remember? No? Well, let me refresh your memory. You took these guns from your man's house, remember?" She waved the loaded .22 in her face. "You knew what that meant. Even if they trace anything, you knew it would lead to him."

Tears escaped her eyes. She felt guilty for dragging her friends into this, acting on her emotions.

"No, no! I can't go to jail for murder. I have a family. This isn't happening again." Cam yanked at her hair and rocked back and forth on the bed.

"She's right, though, Cam," Jaz said, keeping her head down in shame. "We knew what we were doing. We have to move on, and after tonight, we won't ever speak of this again." "What am I supposed to tell my hus—"

"You gon' tell him what you have to and let that be the end of it. I'm sure he won't be that shocked to hear your confessions," Kacey said, letting out a little snicker. Giving up on her attempt to argue, Cam nodded and agreed with her friends. Next morning, everyone woke up feeling different than before, but swore to bury every guilt, regret, and every thought about last night with the murder weapons at the old junk yard.

CHAPTER 8:

THE SEARCH

Jamar gazed out of the plane window, trying to distract himself with the shapes he found in the clouds, but he couldn't shake the feeling something bad had happened—or was about to happen. He hadn't spoken to Jaz in a few days, and he planned to see her as soon as he touched back down in the city. Disrupting his thoughts, the man across from him spoke.

"Mr. Brooks, are you okay? I spoke with your associate Markel, and he mentioned some ideas I feel you would benefit from. With my help, you two could go far," the lawyer, James, said, making conversation.

Once I conclude this business, Markel and I will have a lot of business to discuss, he thought.

"Yeah, I'm fine. How much longer until we arrive?" Jamar said, ignoring his comment about Kel.

James clenched his jaw at the distracted answer, but didn't comment further in favor of sending him a devious smile. "We're actually here."

They exited the plane, and a guy in darkly tinted sunglasses approached Jamar. "Mr. Brooks, if you don't mind, we will need to search you before you enter the building."

"Go ahead," Jamar said, already lifting his arms.

The man patted him down and cleared him before waving him and the other lawyer into the building. Another guard welcomed them at the door and led them to a private elevator at the estate, where his client was waiting for him on the tenth floor.

"Mr. Rogers." Jamar shook his hand. "It's nice to see you again, sir."

"Mr. Brooks, it's always a pleasure. Please, have a seat." He pulled out a chair at the table they sat around. "Now, tell me what's so urgent you needed to see me right away in person." Jamar looked at him with a puzzled expression. "Sir, I was told you asked me to come and meet you in person for an urgent matter."

"Huh?" Mr. Rogers put out his cigar in the ashtray in front of him. "That's strange—" Two shots went off, killing both of Mr. Rogers's bodyguards.

"James, what the hell are you doing?" Mr. Rogers yelled as he looked at his lawyer in disbelief. James held the still-smoking gun in his hand.

"This is me giving you my resignation! I can't work for you anymore—you've become weak! I've been your friend and lawyer for twenty-five years! This is the thanks I get for all those cover ups, pay offs, and time I missed with my family? For what? I told you not to hire this cat; he's taking your money to do nothing in return. You've been dick-riding this little young nigga since the day you met him."

"Have you lost your fucking mind, James? Where is this coming from?" Mr. Rogers shouted as he reached for his tucked .9 mm underneath the table.

"Don't play dumb, motherfucker! I heard you say you were going to leave everything to this nigga, and we all were just supposed to, what, say okay? I could have done everything myself."

"This is the ultimate betrayal. You won't get away with—"

Another shot rang through the room, this time hitting Mr. Rogers in the chest, sending him to the ground. James then turned the gun to Jamar.

"Now, before I end your life, let me tell you this—"

Three bullets went through James's chest. He fell to his knees, clutching his chest and blood-soaked shirt

"W-What?" James choked.

"See, your problem is you're greedy." Jamar lifted himself from his chair and kept his handgun trained on James's weak body. "I saw your shady intensions in our first meeting. You were so anxious to get me here and kill me off that you didn't even notice I replaced your pilot, stewardess, and bodyguards with my own people. You see, that's being smart and tactful," Jamar said before sending one last bullet through his skull.

As Jamar turned to head back to the plane, he heard Mr. Rogers gasping for air, still alive. "I can make you a rich man, Brooks, just get me out of here. You heard him. I'm leaving all this to you in the future."

Jamar started to laugh. "You and your associates have something in common. You're both incompetent. A man should never beg. Also, I'm already rich, and getting you out of the game sooner only makes me richer."

He shot three more bullets into Mr. Rogers, killing him.

* * *

"It's been months. Where could she be? How could she have just disappeared? Jamar thought.

"Are you still thinking about her, bro?" Markel asked as he walked into the large office, seeing Jamar sitting on the edge of a desk, deep in thought.

"Nah," Jamar said too quickly for Markel to believe him. "Why would you think that?" "I can see it all over your face. Don't lie to me."

"Alright, alright, yeah, I am. So what, nigga? She was just different, Kel. For the first time in a long time, she made me feel like myself," he said as he walked around the desk to sit in the replica Iron throne chair.

"It's been over a year; you need to get over that dentist bitch."

"Don't you ever disrespect her, especially in front of me," Jamar said, getting defensive. "Look, all I'm saying is she left without a word, literally overnight, and she still isn't back. She's somewhere, happy with another man, thinking about kids and marriage." "You say that like you know where she is and who she's with."

Markel started coughing after he inhaled too deeply on the joint they were smoking. "Nah, bro," he managed to choke out. "I told you, I had my best guys on it, and they didn't find anything. I know how much she meant to you. I wouldn't do that to you. She's gone, Jay—just let her go."

Jamar was still unconvinced Markel was telling the truth, but he dropped the subject. Markel's bodyguard approached them, holding out a phone. "Sir, it's Ms. Jacks." "Okay, I'll take it." He stood up and grabbed the phone. "Jay, I'll be back." Jamar shook his head and smirked. "Your girl calls and you run out of the room." Markel walked out, but not before giving him the middle finger.

Once Markel left, Jamar frowned, turning his attention to the city view from the office window. He had never met his best friend's girlfriend, and while this wasn't completely uncharacteristic, he was still wary. Markel only referred to her as Ms. Jacks, and always left the room when she called. Jamar couldn't put his finger on it, but he knew something wasn't right. His partner had been acting strange for the last few months, and Jamar was going to find out why.

After a few minutes, Markel walked back in and sat down.

"What was that weird guy's name again, the new client?" Markel asked.

"Quentin D. Pierce. Here's his file." Jamar slid a folder across the table.

"Okay," Kel said as he flipped through the folder, "he's got a clean record. He's new to the city and looking for a partner,"

"He seems *too* clean."

Markel laughed.

"What's so funny?"

"You're overthinking it, bro. He's offering to pay big to work with us. He must have heard how we take care of business."

"But from who?" Jamar asked, suspicious of this man's intentions. "Somebody's talking, and we need to find out who. I think we should meet with him and see what exactly he wants. Markel rolled his eyes.

"I know how this works. This isn't my first rodeo." He left to make the arrangements. Jamar turned his chair back around to the window and daydreamed about Jaz again.

CHAPTER 9:

NEW START

While the sun was coming through the window and shining in Ron's eyes, it still didn't wake him up for work. His blaring alarm would, though. He looked over to see Jaz sleeping peacefully and realized, he had fallen in love with her.

Ron sat up in the bed and buried his head in his hands. *Break it off now; she's dangerous*, he thought to himself. A warm touch across his back and around his chest pulled him from his thoughts.

"Good morning, baby," Jaz said while she kissed him on the neck.

"Hey, baby girl. What're you doing up so early? Go back to sleep; you have a busy day ahead of you."

"I'm up already, Ron. Don't worry about it. Do you want some breakfast before work? You know you need to be alert when you go save lives, officer."

Ron kissed Jaz passionately. "Yes, I'd love some breakfast. Lay back," he said, pushing her back onto the bed.

"But I thought you wanted breakfast?" she asked, giggling like a schoolgirl. Ron spread her legs and teased her with one lick to her pussy. He pressed soft kisses to it, sending chills up Jaz's spine. He kissed her inner thighs and massaged her clit in a counterclockwise motion until she was begging for his fingers to penetrate her. Instead, without notice, he flipped her on her stomach and shoved his penis in her walls from behind. This caused her to lose all control, pushing back on his dick harder and harder while he thrusted into her like a wild dog. They were rough and fast, and their sweat collected on their bodies as their hot pants and moans filled the room. Softly applying the tip of his thumb at the insert of her Ass, mild pressure to let her know he was there.

"Whose pussy is this?" Ron asked and with his free hand he smacked her ass like an African drum when she didn't answer right away. He pounded faster and asked again. "Whose pussy is this?"

"All yours!" Jaz finally screamed out before succumbing to another moan. "I'm coming, Daddy!"

"Me too, baby." Without pulling out, he came inside of her.

They collapsed on each other and enjoyed each other's warmth a moment longer.

Before pulling out and getting out the bed, he whispered in her ear, "Thanks for breakfast."

Daydreaming as she gazed out of the limo window, Jaz wondered what attracted her to Ron. She often wondered if she was settling, dating someone so opposite from her usual tastes. "Jaz, we're here," Milton, her driver and best friend said.

"Thank you, Milton, just give me a minute."

"This house looks amazing every time I pull up to it."

"Thank you, Mil." She smiled. "Please, go on," she teased.

Milton shook his head with a smile. "Girl, this place is amazing. You know that." She laughed. "How'd I get so lucky?" Jaz asked.

"Thank God you met Ron. He's so fine with those damn lips, his thick British accent, and *oo-wee,* don't get me started on them deep-ass dimples."

"Uh, excuse me?" Jaz laughed. This wasn't the first time she'd caught Milton drooling over Ron.

"Oh, my bad." He waved a hand. "Anyway, you're so lucky. You're in a serious relationship, moving into this beautiful mansion with your little perfect poodle."

As if on cue, Cocoa barked.

"I wouldn't be shocked if he asked you to marry him," Milton continued. She raised an eyebrow at him. "Milton, is there something you want to tell me? Did you hear anything?"

"Bitch, I'm not saying anything," he said, smirking.

"I know Ron runs everything by you."

"Duh, I've been your best friend for over three years now, ever since you left the city. But he's paying me very well, so I keep my mouth shut!"

"Damn, you must really like him," Jaz teased.

"Enough to know you two are perfect together. Now, get your cute ass in there and see your man!"

They walked up to the front of the house together.

"Milton, I know you're not keeping my girl hostage, are you?" Ron yelled from the door. Before Milton could respond with something flirty, Jaz yelled, "I'm coming, baby!" She turned to Milton. "Alright, Mil, I'll call you tomorrow about the photo shoot!" She then ran

toward him as Cocoa trailed behind. Jaz dropped her bags before jumping into Ron's arms, kissing him deeply.

Ron placed his hand on Jaz's cheek. "I missed you, baby. How was your day?" "It was very relaxing. Thank you for the spa day. I'm really feeling loose and limber now," Jaz said seductively, placing a warm kiss on his neck.

"That's what I was counting on. Tell Daddy how his girl's pussy's feeling," he whispered in her ear before calling his maid to come get her bags.

"Get in our room and wait for Daddy to return," Ron instructed.

"Okay, Daddy."

He waited until he heard double doors to their room close before he dialed a number on his phone. He spoke quickly in Portuguese, waited to hear two gunshots, and hung up. Back in the room, Jaz was naked on the bed with her back arched and legs spread, waiting for him.

"Come touch me, baby," Jaz moaned.

"No," he said, slowly stepping toward the bed but not sitting. "You're going to touch yourself. Now, wet your fingers and tell me how it tastes."

Jaz obeyed, slowly entering a finger in her pussy and moving it in a slow motion. "Now use two!" Ron demanded, reaching down to unzip his pants, relieving the pressure. She did and moaned louder.

"Put them in deeper." He grabbed his cock the moment she did as she moved her hips up to push them in further. "How does it feel, baby?"

She was barely able to get her answer. "R-Really good, Daddy."

"Daddy can't hear you!" Ron said.

Jaz pushed her fingers in and out of her pussy, faster and faster, while he mimicked her rhythm, pumping his dick into his hand, harder and harder, until they climaxed together.

* * *

"What do you mean you don't think the move was a good decision, girl?" Kacey asked Jaz over their weekly three-way call. "It's been almost three years."

"I keep trying to convince myself it was."

"Look, Jaz, get it together. You know it was for the best, especially after those girls came to your job!"

"Yeah, Jaz, I agree with Kacey—you made the right choice!" Cam agreed from her end. "You're doing so much better out there anyway and—"

"Just stop looking back. Those bitches ended up getting what they deserved anyway." Kacey cut off Cameron and started laughing.

Jaz pulled out her phone and texted Cam privately. *What's up with Kacey lately? She's been more ruthless than usual.*

I know, Cam replied. *I just heard her. She still doesn't give a fuck that she killed those girls. That wasn't even the plan. She took it way too far!*

"Why are you guys so quiet?" Kacey asked. "You hoes side-texting again?" Jaz and Cam laughed uncomfortably because they were caught.

"Girl, I was reading this magazine," Jaz said.

"And I was looking for Kylee and Kaylee."

"Yeah, okay. I have to go anyway. Daddy just got home," Kacey said before trying to end her call with the girls.

"Wait, when are we going to meet this mystery man of yours?" Cam asked. "Never, you hoes!"

They all laughed before hanging up the phone.

* * *

"Who was that, baby?" Markel asked as he walked up behind Kacey and wrapped his arms around her waist. He then moved one hand to her ass and squeezed. Kacey let out a soft moan. "Just the girls, baby. You're home early. Another satisfied client?"

"Yeah, I'm trying to get him to turn on Jamar and work with just me. How about you—?" "You mean work with *us*!" she reminded him with aggression.

"Yeah, once Jamar and Jaz are out of the way, we're going to run this state," he replied. Kacey looked away. She was still not fully on board with Markel and his plan to kill her best friend.

"Markel, I thought we discussed this; I already checked out Jaz. She doesn't know anything. She doesn't even know where Jamar is or if he's even alive. We don't need to kill her. She's my—"

Markel grabbed Kacey by her jaw with so much force she felt like it was going to break if he squeezed any tighter.

"Look, bitch, I told you already. I gave him my word. If Q finds out I lied and betrayed his trust, that could mean we lose everything we're working so hard to build, and I won't lose that just because she's your friend! Remember, friends get you killed! As soon as I take out Jamar, you're taking Jaz out. Do you understand me?"

She hummed in agreement, fearful of doing anything else. He pulled her face close to his and gave her a sloppy kiss.

"Now, get undressed and suck my dick."

Tears rolled down her face as he pushed her to the ground.

CHAPTER 10:

LAST GOOD BYES

"Girls, are you ready?" Cameron asked from the hotel bathroom as she finished her makeup.

"Yes, Mom," Kylee and Kaylee said at the same time.

They headed to the car to start their three-hour drive.

"Before we get there, remember: no talking about the move and what's going on at the house," Cam said to the girls in a serious, firm voice.

The twins looked at each other and tilted their heads down to stare at their shoes. "What's wrong, girls?" she asked. "Talk to me."

"Why can't we stay with Daddy?" Kaylee whimpered.

"Is this really the last time we're going to see Daddy?" Kylee asked.

Cameron felt guilty for even telling them that before their visit. "Look, girls, I will explain when you're older, but for right now, just know this isn't *goodbye*; it's *see you later*." She tried to make her voice cheerier. "Just don't tell Daddy, okay?"

* * *

"Washington!" the guard said at the gate, and buzzed it open to let inmate B265893 in. Sean gave the biggest smile he could fake to his family, knowing he would never see them again. "I swear you two get bigger and bigger every time I see you. I miss you girls." He looked up at his wife. "Cam, you look beautiful."

Her smile was small. "Thank you, baby. I see you cut your hair."

"Yeah, I wanted to try something new." He tried to laugh a little, but it felt forced. He cleared his throat and addressed the girls. "So, what's new? Tell me everything." They told him about school, how they made new friends, and how they'd been keeping their rooms cleaned.

His brow furrowed and stomach turned a moment. "New friends?" Kaylee and Kylee loved their childhood friends, so he wondered why they would make new ones. Cameron added that the girls loved the new things happening in their new life, but she noticed he was distracted.

"Baby, are you okay?" she asked.

"Yeah, I'm fine," he said, lifting his hand up to cradle his head a moment. "Just feeling a little lightheaded. Do you mind asking the guard for a nurse?"

She quickly got up and headed toward the guards.

Sean knew something was going on, something Cam wasn't telling him, but he knew he couldn't ask the girls directly without them telling her. He knew, however, how to get secrets out of them.

"So, Ky, tell Daddy what you learned at the football game."

"Well, I still don't understand it, Daddy. Uncle Terry said to understand football I have to—"

"Oh, Uncle Terry told you that, huh?"

Kaylee jumped in and added. "Yeah, Daddy, and when he moved me, Ky, and Mommy into his big house, he showed us how to do cartwheels in the backyard."

"Wow, really?" Sean was getting everything he needed to know. "When did Uncle Terry move Mommy into his house?" he asked.

"We don't know, Daddy; we weren't there," Kaylee said.

"But I remember when you went away, Daddy, Uncle Terry came over every day, and Mommy said he was your friend and we are all a family now," Kylee chimed. "We miss you, Daddy, and want you to come home and meet our new baby brother." The words pierced his heart. "What baby brother?"

"The one in Mommy's belly. We call him TJ."

Sean's eyes began to water. "Girls, Daddy wants you to go play in the playroom over there so I can talk to Mommy, but first, look at me. I want you girls to know that I will always love you and will always be with you."

With the girls being so young, they didn't really understand what he was saying and that this was their last goodbye.

"We love you too, Daddy, and will see you later," they said in unison as they ran to go play with the games.

Cam came back to the table. "Well, I talked to the nurse and—"

"That wasn't the only person you talked to."

She frowned. "What are you talking about?"

"How are you feeling, Cameron? You have this new vibe to you."

"I'm feeling fine. Why do you ask? Sean, are you okay? I told the nurse to come—" "Shut the fuck up, you lying whore."

Cameron's mouth dropped.

"You're lucky I can't touch you, or you'd be picking yourself off the floor with a broken face. Were you going to tell me you hooked up with my friend and moved the girls to Jersey City?"

"What?" She was so shocked; she was so surprised she couldn't say anything at all. "You think I'm fucking stupid, bitch? You sold the house I bought the girls! When did you start seeing Terry, and before you lie to me, remember I can still make calls to people on the outside. They can take care of shit for me."

Cam couldn't stop the tears falling from her eyes.

"I don't give a fuck about your tears! Tell me how long you've had this prick around my daughters." Sean's voice got louder the angrier he became.

Cam put her head down in shame. "Since you've been locked up, Sean. This was never supposed to happen like this. I was lost without you. When you took the rap for me and the judge gave you that life sentence, I didn't know what to do or think. He came over every day during and after your trial."

"You fucking snake! Why didn't you tell me then that you moved on, Cameron?" He demanded an answer. "I could have moved on too, Cam!" Sean's voice broke. "Are you pregnant, Cameron?"

She sat quiet with her head still down.

"Answer me, dammit!" he yelled, slamming his fists down on the table, causing the family next to them to turn to the scene.

"Yes, I'm five months," she said.

He shook his head. "It all makes since now."

Cameron looked up. "What are you talking about?"

"A few weeks ago, my lawyer said a new witness came forward with evidence that you committed that murder, and they have you on tape."

"What?" Cameron peered around to see if anyone heard. "Sean, you're lying. You're just trying to scare me."

"At this point, Cam, I have nothing to lie about. I pled guilty to your charge and told them it was me and my idea. I couldn't let them take both of us away from the girls. They never took you to court, and they gave me the death penalty. A few days after my visit with my lawyer, I received an anonymous letter saying I should have let you go to jail. The girls could've seen us locked up instead of seeing us both dead. Terry set us up from the beginning. He wanted me out the picture, and you just let him walk right into my shoes. You're weak!"

"Sean, don't say that. You don't know what you're talking about. He's good to us. He's your friend!"

He began to laugh. "That's the point! You're so selfish I hope you rot in hell for what you put me through! You're going to get what you deserve. I did a handful of jobs with this cat, introduced you two maybe twice, and when he started coming over after my lock up, that didn't seem strange to you?"

The guard walked over to their table. "Visiting time is over."

"Yeah, it's been over," said Sean.

The girls ran over to him to get what they didn't know was their last hug. "Daddy, why are you crying?" Kaylee asked.

"Because I love you both. Give me a hug." He kissed his daughters on the forehead and hugged them, none of them wanting to let go.

"Daddy, give Mommy a hug," Kylee said.

"No, Daddy only hugs his family."

"But we are a family," they said, confused.

"Not anymore. Don't forget what Daddy told you guys."

"We'll remember, Daddy."

"We will see you next time, Daddy," Kylee said.

Sean couldn't hold his tears back anymore.

"Don't cry, Daddy. You're going to make us cry," Kaylee said, lip already wobbling. He stared at his two beautiful daughters and tried to remember every detail of their faces, like Kylee's beauty mark on the left side of her face and Kaylee's on her right side. "Visit's over," the guard said again, this time grabbing Sean by his arm and guiding him to the door.

The girls waved to their dad as he disappeared behind the door. Cameron sat at the table, crying.

CHAPTER 11:

THE PLAN

It'd been months since she'd seen Sean, but Cameron was still feeling like her world had ended. She didn't know if she should believe what Sean said, and every time she thought about it, she would get a sharp pain in her stomach. She assumed it was just Braxton Hicks contractions.

"I can't take this huge-ass belly anymore," Cam said to herself in the mirror. She was ready to give birth to her son.

Kylee knocked on the bathroom door. "Mommy."

"Yes?"

"Aunty Kacey is here."

"What? I didn't even hear the doorbell." Cam opened the bathroom door. "How long has she been here?"

Kaylee ran into the room too. "Mommy, Aunt Kacey's here, and she's crying." Cam ran into the living room, holding her belly, and saw Kacey on the couch, sobbing with her head down.

"Girls, go upstairs and let Mommy talk to your aunt."

They did, and Cam sat next to Kacey, rubbing her back.

"What's going on, Kace? What happened? When did you get here? I didn't know you were flying out this weekend. Are you okay?" Cam asked question after question, but Kacey didn't answer. "Look at me, Kacey, and talk to me, dammit!"

Cam gasped as Kacey lifted her head to reveal her blackeye and busted lips. "Who did this to you? Was it that guy you're seeing? Is this why you didn't want us to meet him? I'm going to kill that son of a bitch!"

"Cameron, calm down. Please, it's okay, really, I'm okay."

"No, you're not. Look at your face! If you were okay, you wouldn't look like this and you wouldn't be crying!" She was angry to see her best friend had been physically abused. "When did this happen? How long has this been going on?"

Ashamed, Kacey dropped her head on Cameron's shoulder.

Cam rubbed her back, crying with her. "It's going to be okay, Kace. You're safe now. You're not going back to him. You're going to stay here with us!"

They spent the evening catching up, laughing at the old times. Eventually, Kacey fell asleep while Cam watched TV until Terry came home.

"Baby, where's the—" He was surprised to see Kacey there. "Oh, what's up, girl? When did you get here?"

When Terry saw her face, he started laughing.

Cam threw a pillow at him, waking up Kacey who ran to the bathroom to splash water on her face, and she couldn't help but look up and laugh.

"Great job, baby girl. She fell for everything. I didn't think I was going to be able to hold my laugh. Now it's time to get this in motion. Make me proud," a familiar voice in her head said. She smiled at her reflection before walking out the bathroom.

"Are you feeling better?" Cam asked

"Yes, I'm fine, Mom," Kacey joked.

"Well, good, because you look like shit," Terry said as he walked behind her toward the fridge for a beer.

"Fuck you, Terry." She took the beer from him.

"Nah, you'll need something stronger than that, baby girl." He reached into the cabinet for a bottle of casamigos.

Cam scowled. "That's not what she needs right now."

"No, he's right, Cam. I need a few shots of that." Kacey poured two shots and slid one to Terry.

He looked at Cam. He promised her he wouldn't drink until after the baby got here. "Come on, T!" Kacey urged.

"It's okay, baby, just know your limit," Cam said to him.

Cam wanted Kacey to feel better, so she let her fiancé do this. She watched the two take shots together.

Eventually, due to her swollen feet and tiredness, Cameron was ready for bed. "Okay, baby." Cam got up. "Make sure you eat something! I left some food for you in the oven."

"Thank you, baby." He kissed her and held her close. "Now, go put your feet up and rest." He smacked her ass as she turned to go upstairs.

The majority of the bottle was gone when Terry started to doze off. Kacey remembered why she was here and began massaging his shoulders as she checked behind her to make sure Cam was out of sight.

"So, tell me, Terry, when were you going to stop playing and give me some of that chocolate dick?"

Terry laughed. "Girl, stop playing. Cameron will kill us both. Plus, you can't handle this anaconda."

"Let me be the judge of that," Kacey said. She knelt down and massaged his penis through his jeans.

If he wasn't so drunk, he would've stopped her, but instead, he said, "Stop playing with me and show me what that mouth can do."

He pulled his dick out, and without a pause, Kacey took it all in her mouth, sucking him in with such force he winced from the surge of pleasure. She gripped the base of his penis with one hand and played with her pussy with the other.

"Yeah, bitch, spit on this dick," Terry said as he aggressively forced her head up and down on him with a grip to her hair, and Kacey could feel his movements become more unhinged, so she widened her throat further. He pulled out of her mouth and shot his juice on her face.

Kacey put her head back and accepted every drop.

After he gathered himself, he looked over to Kacey with a smile. "Now, go clean yourself up and get the fuck out of my house. Cameron can't be friends with hoes that sleep with their friend's men."

Kacey was shocked and disgusted, but she got off her knees without saying a word and went to the bathroom to clean up.

Terry dozed off again, but woke up to the sound of a gun being cocked back. "You disrespectful motherfucker. You take your homeboy's wife and get her pregnant after he goes to jail for a crime you paid him to do, and you have the nerve to judge me." Kacey laughed. "This is for Sean, and by the way, his dick tasted better." She put two bullets in his skull.

* * *

"Mommy, wake up!"

Cameron sat up and looked around the room but saw no one. When she glanced over at the time on the nightstand—four in the morning—she noticed Terry hadn't come to bed yet. Suddenly, she felt a sharp pain in her stomach, stronger than anything before. Within seconds, it disappeared. She wasn't due for another five weeks, so she didn't think it was labor contractions. Still, she was concerned.

Cam picked up her cell to call Terry, but it went straight to his voicemail. *He must've fallen asleep drunk again*, she thought. She was irritated, but decided to walk downstairs to bring him to bed. She could hear voices, so she crept along to see who it was. A few steps from the source of the voices, Cameron got the sharp pain again, but this time, she was barely able to stand or talk.

"You know, you shouldn't be out of bed with those swollen feet," a deep, unfamiliar voice said from behind Cameron.

As she turned around, the man gave her a hard punch to the side of her stomach, causing her to fall through the door of the game room and hit her head, knocking her unconscious. "Oh my God, Cameron, are you okay? What happened?" Kacey rushed to her side. "Markel, what did you do?"

Crossing his arms. "This nosey bitch was coming down here, and I just helped her through the door."

Frantically, Kacey tried to comfort Cam. She saw blood pouring out from between her friend's legs. "We need to get her to a hospital. She's not responding."

"We're not going anywhere!" Markel said angrily. "I sent you down here to kill Jaz, not to have a girls' night. And who is this guy you killed with his dick hanging out?"

"His name is Terry. He's her fiancé."

"Okay, why'd you shoot him?"

"He tried to touch me." She was too afraid to admit to the truth.

Markel shot a few rounds into Terry's lifeless body, but unlike Kacey's gun, his didn't have a silencer.

"Kel, that was loud and unnecessary. Why would you do that?" Kacey yelled.

"Because he had it coming. You just got to him before I did." Markel pointed his gun toward Cameron while she was still unconscious.

"No! What the hell are you doing? She's my friend, and she's pregnant."

"She doesn't look pregnant anymore."

The puddle of blood got thicker and spread across the floor.

"Look, bitch," he continued, "you've already got one motherfucker dead, so the way I see it, you have two options: either make this look like a robbery and let's go, or kill her and make it look like self-defense. Whatever you choose, you better choose quick, or I'm choosing for you!"

CHAPTER 12:

WHO'S WHO, WHAT'S WHAT

Jaz was startled out of her sleep by the sound of her phone ringing, and the worst news possible came through from the other end. Cameron was in the hospital. She stumbled out of the bed to get dressed quickly, but knocked some of Ron's boxes from college over. When she went to pick them up, she saw a file with her name on it. Confused but eager to find out what was inside, she opened it and saw photos of Kacey, Cameron, and herself the night they killed those two girls from the office. The file had all their information, including copies of their social security cards, college transcripts, and medical records.

"Jaz!" Milton yelled. He busted through the bedroom door and Jaz tried to stuff the papers back into the box while using the fabric on her shoulders to dry the tears that formed. "What are you doing? We were supposed to leave fifteen minutes ago."

Jaz stood up and tried to act as normal as possible, but her eyes were red and swollen. "What's going on? You look shittier than usual," Milton said, trying to make her laugh, but it didn't work. "What's all this?" He pointed to the loose papers still scattered on the floor. She began crying in earnest now. As she explained, Jaz's phone trilled once more, so Milton picked it up this time in her place, only on the call a few moments before he quickly hung up.

"Jaz, no wonder why you're crying." He hugged her. "We really need to go, though. They said Cam just got out of surgery."

Jaz nodded, relieved her friend was okay, and the two of them left.

* * *

Kacey sat in the waiting room, still covered in blood, rocking back and forth. "Kacey, what are you doing here? What happened to you? Why are you covered in blood?" Jaz asked.

"It happened so fast, Jaz. He was trying to touch me, and I screamed," Kacey said, voice cracking.

Jaz's stomach dropped.

"Cam heard me, but he pushed her. He started hitting me, then he reached for his gun and shot Cameron. I managed to get the gun away from him, and I shot him. It was self-defense."

Jaz couldn't believe what she was hearing. "Wait, Terry? I can't believe this! Where are the girls? Did they see any of this?"

"No, they were in bed."

"Why were you and Terry alone? What were you doing at Cam's house?" Jaz asked. "How did you even—" Jaz was cut off by the nurse.

"Washington family?"

"Yes, that's us."

They ran over to the doctor.

"How is she doing? Can we see her? How is the baby?" Jaz asked so quickly, not even giving the doctor time to answer.

"Ma'am, calm down, please. As for Mrs. Washington, she's out of surgery. The bullet grazed her skull, causing a lot of swelling. She's in a coma, and we aren't sure when she'll wake up. All we can do now is wait."

"Where is the baby? Can I see him?" Jaz asked again.

There was a pause before he said, "I'm sorry, we couldn't save the child." A sob escaped her chest. "No, no, no. This can't happen. She didn't even decide on a name."

"I'm sorry for your loss," the doctor said and walked away.

Jaz cried on Kacey's shoulder. A nurse turned the corner and approached the group. "Ms. Evans, can I speak to you alone for a minute?" Jaz followed her over to an empty hallway as kacey sat back in her chair.

"Do you know me or something?"

She shook her head. "Only from pictures and stories at her prenatal visits. I'm Cam's friend. She speaks about you a lot. Cam had to be put into an induced coma, but before surgery, she wouldn't stop screaming your name."

"I didn't do this. I wasn't—"

She lifted up a hand. "Your alibi has been confirmed by police. Don't worry. I overheard them talking about it."

"Okay." Jaz was hesitant.

"I'm worried about Cam's safety and the safety of her girls."

"What do you mean?"

"When Cameron was rushed to the hospital, your friend Kacey came in with her. I saw she had a few bruises and scrapes, so I asked how she acquired the wounds." "She was attacked like our friend Cameron by the same guy, right?"

The woman peered over Jaz's shoulder to make sure they were still alone before turning back to her. "I don't believe that is true."

"Why not?" she asked.

"Well, it's not my place to say, but the wounds on her face don't match what she said happened. The blackeye and cut lip look like they're from a few days prior." "But she was covered in blood."

"Yes, the blood on her clothes and arms are fresh, and it looks like it was placed on her intentionally, and—"

She gasped. "What?"

"I think this attack was planned and Kacey was in on it."

Her eyes filled with tears. She couldn't believe what she was hearing.

"The police want to talk to you. You are listed as Cameron's next of kin and the girls' legal guardian. I'm scared for these girls because they saw everything their mother endured last night. They were awake, and I'm afraid something will happen to them because of what they may have seen."

"Where are they?" Jaz asked.

"Still with CPS, probably waiting for you. Be careful, please."

Jaz hugged the nurse. "Thank you for everything!"

"Just keep those girls safe," she said, wiping her tears. She retreated back to the nurse's station.

* * *

It'd been weeks since Cameron's accident, but she still hadn't woken up. Jaz hadn't talked to Kacey since then. Despite not wanting to believe it, she knew Kacey was involved somehow. She'd spent that time with the girls at her home she shared with Ron. "Aunt Jaz, are you okay?" Kylee asked.

Jaz was caught off guard. She'd been throwing as many things into her duffle bag as she could fit. She didn't know where they were going, but Jaz knew she needed to get out of the city and fast.

"Hey, baby girl." She hugged her. "Yes. I'm fine. How about we take a girls trip?" Excited for their mystery trip, the girls screamed with glee.

"But I need you to do me a favor first," Jaz continued.

"Yes?"

"I want you and your sister to go pack all the clothes you want to bring with you." The girls were excited.

"Maybe we're going to go see Daddy," Kaylee said.

"No, maybe we're going to go see our new baby brother," Kylee told her as they both raced off to the room they'd been sleeping in.

Jaz felt horrible; the girls had no idea. She buried her head in her knees. *"Cameron, I'm sorry for everything. I wasn't there for you, but I swear I'll keep the girls safe."*

* * *

Ron dialed Jaz's number.

"Hey, baby, I've been calling you all morning. Where are you? Are you okay?" Ron asked over the phone.

She wasn't sure if she should tell him about Cameron and how they were taking her off life support, or her suspicions about Kacey.

"Jaz, can you hear me?"

"We're all packed," Kylee yelled from downstairs.

"Baby, talk to me," Ron said. "Did I just hear one of the twins? Is Cam awake?" She brushed away the tears gathering in her eyes. "I'm here, baby, and yes, that was Ky. I'm taking the girls out for a little. Can I call you back?" Jaz finally responded. She was trying to rush Ron off the phone before he figured out she was lying.

"You sound upset. How about we take the girls—"

"Look, Ronald, I'm already running late and the girls want to go."

"Something's up. I can tell. I can meet you guys wherever you're going."

"No!" Jaz yelled then said quieter, "No, thank you. I'll just talk to you later, okay? We can all meet for lunch," she said and hung up.

Something didn't sit right with Ron. He knew Jaz always had her phone on her, so it didn't make sense that she wouldn't call him. He decided to get in contact with Milton. "Hey, Milton. It's Ron," he said when Milton answered the phone.

"Have you talked to Jaz? I can't get ahold of her," he lied. He knew Milton would tell him everything.

"I actually just dropped Jaz and the girls back off at the house. We came from the hospital. They decided to pull the plug on Cam today. The girls still have no idea that Terry was murdered. Jaz has full custody of the kids now."

Ron couldn't believe Jaz didn't tell him this.

"Hello? Ronald, are you still there?"

"Uh, yeah. Thanks, Mil, but I have to go," he said and hung up the phone.

* * *

Jaz's phone rang again.

"Ron, stop calling my damn phone. I said—"

"Uh, Jaz?" Kacey laughed on the other end of the phone.

"Sorry, Kacey, I didn't even look to see who was calling before I picked it up." "Where are you? I haven't seen you since the hospital. I know the girls are with you." "Yeah, my bad. I've just been busy getting things together with the girls." "Yeah, I had to rush out that day too anyway. I had things to do."

"Kacey, our best friend lost her unborn child, and her fiance just died! What could you have possibly had to do?" Jaz was done with Kacey.

"Are you kidding me, Jaz?" Kacey giggled. "This wasn't her first time losing a Man." Jaz was at a loss for words. She just shook her head and said, "You need help, Kacey." "I really do," she agreed, pausing a moment before suggesting, "Let's meet up and talk about it."

"Okay, meet me at Cameron's house."

"I'll see you in an hour," Kacey said before hanging up.

CHAPTER 13:

THE TRUTH

What could Markel possibly be doing in this area? Jamar thinks to himself as he sat watching a few houses back from the house he followed him to.

He'd been watching the house for a few minutes now, trying to figure out what Markels plan. A yellow taxi pulled up in front of the house, and a familiar-looking woman got out and entered the house.

"Damn, he's just getting some pussy, and I'm looking crazy," Jamar said to himself and laughed. He put his gun back on safety and tucked it under the seat.

A few moments later, another woman in a red Range Rover with lashes on the headlights pulled into the driveway. He scoffed and rolled his eyes at the ridiculous decoration before reaching to start his midnight-blue Hellcat.

"My boy's about to have an orgy." He laughed to himself again until he saw who was getting out of the car: Jaz.

Jamar watched her walk in the house, and quickly, he pulled his gun from under the seat. Sweating bullets now, he waited until nobody was outside to jump out of the car and crouch down low. His heart raced. He wondered why she was here with Markel. He felt so betrayed that Markel lied to him.

* * *

"Hello? Kacey, are you here?" Jaz called as she opened the door. "Why is it so damn dark in here?"

"Yeah, Jaz, I'm in the back. Come on in."

"Bitch, why are you acting so weird? Why did you want to meet—"

She was cut off by a blow to the head.

"What the fuck, Markel? Why'd you hit her so hard?" Kacey asked, running from the back into the front room.

"That bitch deserved it for making us wait," he said and tossed the weapon to the side. Kacey rushed to check Jaz's head. "She's bleeding. I need to get her a towel." "No! Leave her!" Markel said.

"She's my friend and—"

"No, she isn't. Pick her ass up and put her in the chair. Tie her wrists too." Kacey did, though reluctantly, and when she was done, Markel bent down to be at eye level with Jaz.

"Hey, wake up!" He slapped her across the face. "Wake up, bitch!"

Jaz's eyes flickered open.

"Well, hello, sunshine. It's nice of you to join us," Markel teased.

"What happened? Where am I?" Jaz asked, starting to come to with a few slow blinks. "You're asking the wrong questions," he said, standing back up.

When she realized what was happening, her heart sped up. "Why am I tied up? Who are you? Where is Kacey?"

"Damn, you're a curious one. I see why he liked you."

"Who?" Jaz asked. She studied his face. "I've seen you somewhere."

Markel hit Jaz again, causing her to scream.

"Alright, that's enough," a deep voice said from the corner of the room.

Jaz looked up. "If I wasn't tied up, your bitch ass wouldn't be so tough. Let me go and let's have a fair fight, or kill me now!"

A laugh came from the dark corner of the room. "You've always been feisty. That's one of the things I loved about you, Jaz."

She gasped. "Dukes?"

He stepped into the light. Even after all this time, she still recognized him. "I thought you died in that shootout a few years ago. What the fuck are you doing? Why are you doing this?"

"There are the million questions again. It's been years, and that's all you have to say to me?"

"Am I supposed to be happy to see you? You're fuck-ing insane! Dukes, are you behind Cameron's attack? Where is Kacey?"

"That's a question you should ask your girl about." He turned to Markel. "Tell your bitch to come out and stop hiding."

"Baby, come here," Markel yelled.

Kacey walked in slowly with her head down. She started sobbing when she saw Jaz.

"Jaz, listen, everything happened so fast," Kacey explained. "I didn't know they were working together, Du—"

Shots pierced the air, bullets flying everywhere, and Jaz shrieked as windows shattered. Jaz tipped over the chair, falling to the ground, and she managed to untie her wrist earlier while Dukes was talking. Once she was completely free, she darted behind a couch, trying to avoid the flying bullets. Peeking her head around the couch, she tried to find Kacey through the gunfire. She looked up to see where some of the shots were coming from, and across the room she saw Jamar. They locked eyes and he mouthed, "*Stay there, baby, I'm coming to you.*" He leapt then rolled across the large door frame to her, the bullets only missing him by an inch as it splintered the cherry wood frame. Dukes and Markel used the overturned dining table as cover. Kacey crawled on her stomach across the floor into the next room and hid behind the door. "Jamar? What are you doing here?"

"Jaz, baby, I can't believe you're here. You just disappeared. Why did you—" "We don't have time for questions. We can talk later. You still pack the Guppie on your right leg?"

Jamar looked up and smiled. "You know I do, baby girl."

"Good. We're going to need it." They both jumped from behind the door, letting off shot after shot, and fell into the bathroom. Jaz kicked the door closed behind them. Jamar sat up against the bathtub and looked at his bleeding wound. The bullet had hit the femoral artery. Blood quickly soaked his sweater.

Jamar tried to stand but collapsed back down.

"Okay, baby girl, you're going to have to find a way out and go get us some help." Jaz took her attention away from the door, hand still gripping her gun, and she dropped to the floor beside him to cover his wound with her free hand.

"No, I'm not as delicate as you think! I'm getting us out of here, and these motherfuckers are going to die today! Do you trust me?" she said as she looked at him with love, lust, and passion. Jamar felt his heart skip a beat. Even seeing her with the scrapes, cuts, and bruising on her face, he still thought she was the most beautiful being. "Yes, baby, I trust you." He cocked back his pistol, gripping his wound.

Using Jamar's spare gun, Jaz stood tall and went through the door like lightning, firing shot after shot. Jamar's eyes lit up. He loved seeing his woman handle business like this. The bullets tore through Dukes, and he fell against the wall with a blood trail following his body.

After the volley of shots quieted, Jaz yelled, "Jamar, are you good?"

"I think we got them all."

She ran back to Jamar in the bathroom.

"Drop the guns, Bonnie and Clyde! Looks like you missed, bitch!" Markel said, appearing before them with bullet wounds in his shoulder.

Jamar was furious beyond words. "Your snake ass doesn't deserve to live!" "You think you do? We've both done shit we're not proud of. What makes this different?" Markel asked. "Oh, wait, it's this bitch, huh?" He pointed his gun at Jaz and turned his attention toward her. "You just didn't get the message to stop fucking with him, even after I sent those bitches to your job. All you had to do was leave town quietly, but you brought your girls into it. How does it feel to kill again, Jaz? Kacey told me how easy it was for you." "What is he talking about, Jaz? Is this why you left without saying anything?" Jamar asked.

CHAPTER 14:

THE END OF
THE BEGINNING

"Honestly, Jaz, that was some gangster shit you pulled," a familiar voice from behind said.

A man walked through the door, and before Jaz could say anything, Jamar stuttered his name.

"R-Ronald, is that you? Where have you been? I've been looking for you!" Jaz was confused. "Ron, what are you doing here? How did you find me?" "Jaz, sweetheart, I always know where you are. I placed a tracker in your necklace I

bought you for Christmas. I know this all seems weird, but I can explain," said Ron. Markel pointed the gun at Jamar, but Ron was quicker. Jaz closed her eyes as she heard three shots go off. A body dropped to the floor; it was Markel's.

"He really thought I was going to let him live." Ron laughed. standing in front of her "Look, Jaz, let me explain everything, and you'll start to see things clearer. I have to start from the beginning."

"Jaz, don't listen to him. He's a liar and—"

Ron shot a bullet into Jamar's leg.

"Now, can I continue, please? You know I used to hate when you interrupted." "How do you know each other?" Jaz asked.

"He's my dear ol' big brother," he answered with a false cheer.

"But you're from London!" she screamed in anger.

"I'm not just a traffic cop—I actually work undercover for MI5. I've been watching you since before we officially met. I know all about what you, Kacey, and Cameron did that night before you fled the city."

After seeing the files, Jaz had suspected this already.

"I did fall in love with you, though, so I'm going to offer a deal that will let you walk free right now." Ron got down on one knee on the blood-soaked carpet. "Ja'kahlii Eynette Williams, I have lied and killed for you, and I've protected you since the day I met you. Will you do me the honor of becoming my wife?" He held out a diamond ring.

Jaz was overwhelmed and unable to comprehend what was happening.

"Answer my questions truthfully, and I will accept your hand in marriage." She just wanted to know what was going on.

"Of course, baby, whatever you need, but then you have to kill Jamar."

He handed her a gun, after she had dropped Jamar's empty spare, and she hesitated for a few moments before she took it. She knew this was the only way to get back to Kaylee and Kylee alive.

"Why me?" Jaz asked. "I don't understand why this is all about me."

"There is nothing more satisfying than taking the one thing your most hated enemy cherishes. Jamar always got everything as a boy, but then I got to have you." "Do you even love me?" Jaz cried.

"Of course I grew to love you, Jaz."

"How did you find me?"

"A few years ago, I was on an assignment listening to a wiretap for local drug and arms dealers that had been crossing over to the UK without paying the fare. The cat's name was Quincy Dukes Pierce." He pointed to Dukes dead body in the corner. "He spoke about planning a murder and kidnap. Once I started going through case files, I found Markel was one of his connected errand boys. He was a childhood friend of my brother's. I started investigating Markel's pending murder and drug charges and I found a photo of this guy." He turned his attention back to Jamar and squeezed his bullet wound, causing him to yelp out in pain. "We were young when our mother overdosed, they separated us. Soon after, I was adopted by a British family, and we left the states to London. Once I reached eighteen, I began my search, but it wasn't until my career that I could actually find Jamar. Once I knew about Markel, I knew he would lead me to him. It would only take a matter of time. It was easy to turn Markel. He was motivated by money and greed. I found out Dukes linked with Kel after he found out where you were, Jaz. He was still in love with you."

None of these moments felt real to Jaz. She felt faint, and her stomach started to churn. She turned her head, unable to hear anymore.

"It was just my luck when I decided to follow you that night after your attack, to find you and your girls dumping those bodies. I now had all the pieces in place. Markel got Kacey's trust after he paid those dumb ass thugs to stage her kidnapping and car jacking that night, and that brings us here," Ron explained.

Jaz processed all of this.

"I'm telling you, here and now, I love you, and my brother doesn't deserve you!"

Out of nowhere, Kacey ran from behind and grabbed the gun from Ron. She thought she was successful, but Ron overpowered her and threw her onto the floor over broken glass, which ripped through her skin like paper. "It's a shame your friends have always lived the life you wanted," Ron said, standing over Kacey. "You got the chance to take it away from them, but now you look foolish. You trusted this dumbass." He pointed his gun toward Markel's body. "He used you the same way everyone has always used you! You're stupid and useless." Ronald kicked her in the stomach.

"Leave her alone!" Jaz screamed out. "Please, stop. I can't lose another friend." Ronald knelt down to Kacey. "Did you tell your best friend all of your secrets?" He tilted his head back toward Jaz's direction.

Kacey remained quiet.

"Today is going to be the day you confess to all of your sins." He stood up and pointed the gun at Kacey. "Confess, bitch!"

"Jaz, I'm sorry. I haven't been the best friend you two deserved."

"You're going to have to do better than that. Tell her why you don't deserve any sympathy." Ron shot a bullet through her foot, and she screeched.

"Please, just leave her. Whatever she's done, I don't care. Kacey, I don't care! I love you, and you will always be my sister," Jaz pleaded.

"It's adorable that you see the good in everyone, but this deceitful bitch doesn't have any good in her!" Ron stepped on her wound.

"I did it!" Kacey screamed. "I killed Terry!"

"And?" Ron stepped harder on her foot.

"When Cameron came downstairs, I shot her too."

Jaz couldn't believe what she heard.

"I'm the reason we're here. I helped set this up! I knew Jamar was still looking for you! I knew Dukes planned to kill you! But I didn't know Ron was secretly working with them." She continued to sob. "I'm sorry, Jaz. I love you and Cameron forever."

Ron emptied his clip into Kacey's skull.

Jaz realized she was alone in this world and would be stuck with Ron. She couldn't live in fear, so she whirled around and unloaded three bullets into Ron's chest before she realized what she was doing. He collapsed to the floor.

"You know something, Ronald," she said to his dying body. "I always knew I'd break your heart, but I never thought it would be literally."

Jaz walked over to Kacey's body. "You will always be my sister. I'm sorry I couldn't help you in the way you needed."

She remembered Jamar and ran over to him. "You better not die on me, you selfish bastard. I just got you back."

"I never stopped missing you," he said. "But, baby, I just need to know one thing." She was afraid of what it might be.

"When did you become so gangsta?" He tried to laugh but it was painful. "I'll explain everything after we get out of here!"

They left the house, and she helped Jamar into her vehicle. She swerved in and out of traffic to get back to the house.

"Jamar, stay with me. You're going to be okay. We're almost there."

She could hear him struggling to breathe.

"Baby, stay with me. Talk to me. Tell me something beautiful."

"You," he managed to utter.

Tears formed in her eyes, streaking down her cheek.

The car became quiet.

Jaz knew he was special. She continued to drive home and rolled down her windows. She heard the sounds of seagulls.

Jamar couldn't feel his wounds anymore. He saw a bright light and heard a familiar voice. He wanted to hear more, so Jamar allowed himself to fall into a deep sleep. With his last breath he said, "Goodbye, Jaz. Hello, Mom."

REVENGE FANTASIES:

Part 2

He stared at her before leaning over to whisper what he planned to do to her that night. Her heart skipped a beat, and she moved in for a breathtaking kiss. When he pulled away, she whispered, "Get on top." She kissed his neck. "I'm ready for you to have me." He looked down at her then asked, "Are you sure?"

"Yes." She smiled.

That was when it got real. He put her on her back then kissed her slowly, starting from her brown full lips, then to her neck. He snuck a hand underneath the hem of her shirt, and she jumped at the feel of his cool hands on her body.

"Sorry, babe. They'll warm up soon," he said in a silky voice as he inched his way to her breast, making her wet between the legs. Feeling the shirt bunching up, she paused, debating whether she should take it off.

Noticing her hesitation, he asked, "Are you sure you're ready? We can wait, beautiful. You're worth it."

Hearing that, she smiled and shook her head. "No, I'm ready." With that, she shucked off the shirt and smirked at the way he admired her curvy body sans bra. She was a little thicker than most, but she was proud of that and was happy he was too.

He commented again on her beauty, then moved to slide up the expanse of skin from her stomach to her breasts. She sucked in a breath when he skated over her nipples, so in response he pinched one. She moaned and moaned even further when he took his other hand to caress her through her purple lace panties. Lifting her hips up, he helped her take them off, where they fluttered to the floor. She widened her legs for him, and he pushed one finger in. She gasped, so he dropped a soft kiss to her thigh.

"First experience is always strange," he said then went in and out slowly. "Are you ready for two?"

Shakily, she nodded, biting her lip, but another moan escaped her as he added in another. Her hips jumped up to meet his hand, but when he noticed her face, she was close to climaxing, so he stopped, and she let out a whimper.

"Want a taste?" he asked, bringing his fingers up to her mouth, and she latched on, swirling her tongue around, and he met her mouth with his as soon as she was done.

Pushing her back, he spread her legs and positioned himself at her entrance.

"This will hurt for a few minutes, but it will get better, I promise."

Seeing the sincerity in his eyes, she said, "I trust you."

The tip of his dick moved across the front of her pussy lips, and she kissed him as he slowly pushed inside of her. She whimpered, so he paused.

"Do you want me to stop?"

Taking in a deep breath, she said, "No, no, it'll get better. You promised."

Nodding, he pushed in deeper, taking pains to go as slow as possible. Once he finally heard her say, "Harder and faster," that was when pounded into her. She wrapped her legs around his back and moaned his name, and he climaxed inside her.

* * *

"Where have you been all night?" Kaylee asked Kylee as she snuck through their bedroom window.

"You know our mom is dead, right? You don't get to question me," Kylee snapped back.

"Yeah, don't forget you were born nine minutes and nine seconds before me too," Kaylee mocked Kylee, making air quotations at what she knew her sister was about to say next as she always did in arguments. They both laughed.

"I know you're just worried about me, Lee-Lee, but you know I could have been with only one person." Her voice was sincere.

Kaylee focused her attention to her sister. "So, did you guys finally do it?"

Kylee ducked her head down

"What happened? Are you okay? Did he do something you didn't like? Talk to me!"

Kylee looked up, cheesing from ear to ear. She loved playing with her sister, knowing she was so sensitive when it came to her.

"Yes, we did, and it was amazing! He was so patient with me. He held me, took his time with every part of my body, and it was perfect," she reminisced with sigh.

"You shouldn't play like that, Ky! You gon' be the little bitch who cried wolf one day!" She tried to keep up her attitude up toward her sister, but she couldn't contain her excitement any longer.

"O-M-G, Ky, you're a woman now! I cannot believe you did it. I'm just glad it was with somebody you love. Are you going to tell Aunty?"

"Fuck no! I tell her, and she'll kill us both," Kylee responded nervously.

"Why both of us? I'm not the one out here licking and sticking! You are."

Kylee placed her hand on her sisters' shoulders. "Now, you *know* Aunty Jaz gon' give us the 'We're supposed to always be together' speech. Then she's going to ask why I snuck out and you didn't tell her. And then she might beat both our asses for keeping secrets from her."

Knowing her sister was completely right, Kaylee laughed, Kylee joining in.

When they settled, Kylee poked her sister in the shoulder and said, "You're asking me about my personal life, but the real question is, are you going to tell Aunty how you'd rather eat a taco than a sausage?"

"My sexuality shouldn't be so hilarious, Kylee. I love Stephani," she said as she walked toward the door, trying to end the oncoming conversation her sister was trying to have with her, but upon opening their bedroom door, Santana fell through the doorway as he attempted to eavesdrop. Kaylee hit him with a shoe jokingly.

"What we tell you about listening in on conversations, you little punk?"

Kylee crowed Santana into the dresser behind him.

"If you repeat any of this to Aunty, that's your ass and I'm the lawnmower! You got me?"

He nodded frantically, and his eyes watered. She smacked him on the side of his head and made a scat noise for him to leave. He ran out, yelling for his mom and crying.

Not a full three minutes went by before there was knocking on the door.

"Good morning, Aunty Jaz," The twins said in unison.

That always gave Jaz butterflies. She couldn't believe how big they'd gotten so fast. Kylee made a snapping gesture in front of Jaz face.

"Oh yeah, why did you girls make Tana cry? You know that kid's sensitive like his daddy."

"Aunty, he's sensitive cause he's both y'all's child," Kaylee joked.

Poking his head through the other side of the door, Jamar said, "You know I heard all of that, right...?"

EPILOGUE

Hey Everyone, Its Jess! I Just wanted to take this time after that nail-biting crazy plot twist Ending I left you guys with to say thank you from the bottom of my heart for taking the time out to not only purchase my book but actually reading it! Before I get into all the emotional reasons why I'm grateful for you all, I want to take a moment to zoom in on one of the Key and most important sections of my book that hit a little close to home. One of The Fictional Characters I created named Kacey Suffers from a severe case of schizophrenia which she tries to suppress. There could have been multiple reasons why kacey couldn't confide in her mother for help and address it from an earlier age. I have a family member who also suffers from this condition and refuses to get proper medical attention, everyday they're a new more aggressive less passive person. My family and i have given so much to help achieve a healthy productive life, but everyday brings a new challenge for all of us. All this brings me to say if you or someone you know are affected by this illness, don't not give up on them and don't give up on yourself! There are multiple help centers in every major city, www.psychiatry.org, www.nasmhpd.org, www.montarebehavioralhealth.com. Just a few resources that could help in many ways like it has done for us. Prayer Before Progress. #LetsBreakTheCycle